The GREENING of LARRY MAHON

Dave Duggan

*With best
wishes,*

Dave Duggan

GW00401800

LONG
TOWER
A Long Tower book from
GUILDHALL PRESS

For information on the Penan and their struggles contact:
Survival International
6 Charterhouse Buildings
London EC1M 7ET
www.survival-international.org

First published in November 2004
Guildhall Press, Unit 15, Ráth Mór Centre,
Bligh's Lane, Derry BT48 0LZ
T: (028) 7136 4413 F: (028) 7137 2949
info@ghpress.com www.ghpress.com

ISBN 0 946451 81 8

Cover design by Mark Willett
Typesetting by Kevin Hippsley

Supported by the Arts Council of Northern Ireland

This Project is supported by the European Union, administered by the
Local Strategy Partnership for the Derry City Council Area.

**EU Programme
for Peace and Reconciliation**
in Northern Ireland and the Border Regions of Ireland

**ARTS
COUNCIL**
of Northern Ireland

LOCAL STRATEGY PARTNERSHIP
DERRY CITY COUNCIL AREA

About The Author

Dave Duggan is a writer and director. His stage plays, *The Peace Process Trilogy*, *Scenes from an Inquiry* and *The Recruiting Office*, produced by Sole Purpose Productions, have been variously seen in Ireland, New York, Liverpool and at The Edinburgh Fringe. The Playhouse, Derry, produced *Spike Dreams* for a national tour. BBC Radio 4 and RTÉ Radio 1 have produced his radio plays, *From a Great Height*, *The Man with no Ears*, *Scenes from an Inquiry*, *Joe S'againne* and *The Blackbird's Last Campaign*. His film and video work, for Raw Nerve Productions, includes *Cú Chulainn*, *Tumbleturns* and the Oscar-nominated *Dance Lexie Dance*. Lagan Press publish his *Shorts for Stage and Screen*. Originally from Waterford, Dave lives in Derry. This is his first novel.

For Fiona and Brian
Grá i gcónaí

PART ONE

Forest

CHAPTER ONE

The Penan came out of the forest and stood across the road as the Land Rover slewed through the mud. There were men with parangs, others with blowpipes and women with babies on their backs. They stood in the driving rain, impressive in their quietness.

Ilpe wound down his window and shouted at them as he braked to a slithering halt. 'Geta the fuck outa road,' he shouted, his English laced with American slang and profanities. He shouted again, this time in pidgin Malay and finally in Tagalog. Still the Penan did not move.

Then Arkland's voice came over the radio, full of cackle and hiss.

'Where are you, Ilpe? Call in now. Over.'

'Penan here, boss. All over the road. Bastards never learn. Over.'

'Put Mahon on. Over.'

Ilpe handed me the mouthpiece. I was tired. I really needed a break from all this. 'Mahon here. We'll get through. Just take it easy. It's always like this. Over and out.'

As if they'd heard me, the human barricade opened, leaving a path for us. Ilpe gunned the Land Rover into life, released the brake, threw on the four-wheel drive and we lunged forward through the mud. I heard my theodolite, free of its lashings, slap against the body of the Land Rover. A boy ran out from behind his mother, her arms flaying the air as she tried to catch him. I shouted 'Stop' as Ilpe found second gear and we slewed forward.

I lost sight of the boy and then suddenly I saw his startled eyes looming on our left side and I heard the sickening squelch as we drove on. I shouted 'Stop' again, but Ilpe just drove on, his face thrust forward, his knuckles blanching on the steering wheel. I thought he must have gone mad. I looked at him, convinced he had flipped. His brown face was drained, his knuckles gleamed white on the steering wheel. But he drove on.

A dumper truck moving loggers came towards us after we rounded the next bend and we had to stop to let it pass. I jumped out of the Land Rover into the mud and squelched my way to the edge of the road. I had engineered this stretch nearly a year before and it always gave me pleasure to see how well it was holding up. The culverts were taking the rain off. There had been no slips over the edge. As the rain pounded my bare head, I concentrated on these professional concerns until the startled eyes of the boy forced their way back into my mind.

The human barricades had become so much a part of my workaday life that I hardly thought about them any more. There was never any violence, just quiet groups of people in ragged shorts, who made their protest, then let us pass.

I looked across the valley at the hillsides covered in forest. They were part of our concession, but we hadn't reached them yet. I called up images of the dripping leaves and the sodden lianas dangling from the top layers miles above the forest floor, where I often stood ankle deep in rotting vegetation.

The rainforests enthralled me in a way nothing – no man, no woman, no loyalty, no patriotism, no cause – ever had. I had no ambition other than to work in these great forests, these last outposts of the human crusade through the natural world.

Then the boy's eyes came back to me, and the sickening squelch as we had driven on. I smelled rotting flesh, not vegetation, and it was rancid in my nostrils. I walked back to the Land Rover, hoping Ilpe had come to his senses. I noticed that some colour had at least come back into his face. He was Filipino, reared near the US Army base at Subic Bay on the island of Luzon. He'd come over from Sandakan when we opened the new timber concession a year before, in early 1991.

'We go on?' he asked.

'No,' I said. 'We go back.'

He turned the Land Rover, expertly slewing and braking in

the mud, and drove back towards the camp. I asked him to stop at the spot where the Penan had been, and I got out again. The rain had eased, though it hadn't stopped. It would go on like this for hours.

There was no-one around. No footprints. No sign whatsoever of the human barricade or the boy. I floundered around in the mud. It was streaked red with the boy's blood. More blood glistened in small pools of water. I walked to the edge and looked over the valley again. The hills opposite were almost completely hidden in cloud, and a muffled rumble of thunder echoed around me. It was metallic-dark, and then the rain grew heavy again and the ground slipped under me. I looked down to see the edge cracking and loosening and I stepped back in time to see clods of earth lift away and slip down into the valley with a shudder.

Ah, Lawrence. Yes. A grand lad. Very bright always. Loves the travel but. Loves it. Breaks his mother's heart that he's away. First it was the Amazon, then Cameroon, then a wee stint in Australia, and now Borneo. Borneo, if you don't mind. The wild man, eh? Ah, yes. His mother misses him terrible. Will he ever come home? Naw, I don't... Take something big. See, he loves out foreign, like.

My father's voice needled me. Why had he come into my head just as the earth slipped from under me? Thoughts of home came to me as death touched me. Guilt. Was that why the ground slipped under me? Was it?

'I wasn't driving,' I repeated to myself as I climbed back in the Land Rover. 'Ilpe was.'

Ach, there's nothing here for him, you know. He's over-qualified I suppose. Loves the forests out there. Used to send us photos, the first trip especially. The wife has them in an album. She doted on him. The eldest, you see.

My father again, a voice in my head, clearer than ever now. Ilpe stared at me and I just nodded. I said nothing to him as we drove back to the camp. I hid inside my head, trying to push away the vision of the boy's eyes, but the only images strong enough to do that were images of home. I didn't know which was worse.

Arkland was standing on the verandah outside his office as

we drove up. He was wearing shorts, a T-shirt, heavy boots and a gigantic sou'wester. Ilpe pulled up in front of the wooden block that held the secure lock-up as well as Arkland's and my offices, large spare rooms which connected to our personal quarters.

'Come into the office,' he said. We followed him as he dragged his shattered left leg behind him. I couldn't take my eyes off the weals and the scars.

'Anti-personnel device. Doesn't do it justice somehow,' he'd once told me. He'd had the leg propped on the rail of the verandah. It was dark and the cicadas were screeching. We were drinking Jack Daniels he'd brought back from a trip to the capital. We were solemnly drunk.

'A small explosive device and a shit load of rusty nails, bits of wire and maybe old tin cans. A Viet Cong speciality. You step on one of a million twigs and whazzam, your leg's blown to bits. Your buddies are too stoned on Laotian Red to know you've been blasted and the surgeon – who finally carves you up – says he came close to not being able to save the leg. Kinda wish he hadn't, sometimes.'

Arkland told me he never went home after Vietnam. He'd been in US Special Forces there and he was still fiercely strong and fit despite the damaged leg.

'Take more than some gook bomb to slow old Arkland down. Hell, they can have the other leg and I'm still better than ten of them,' he'd said.

In the office, Arkland took off his sou'wester and waved us into chairs. He slipped into his own chair, keeping his left leg stuck out in front of him.

'What happened?'

The question was for me, but I felt Ilpe should really be answering it. I looked across at the Filipino driver and he returned my stare. I was the engineer. I was the company man. I would have to answer.

'There was a Penan barricade at Kilometre Ten or so. Usual sort of thing. Except I think we ran over a boy.'

'You think?'

'Yes. I think. I'm not sure. It was hard to be sure.'

I was sure. The boy's eyes kept racing across the front of my mind. I just didn't want to say it out loud.

Arkland pushed himself out of his chair and limped over to the wall maps. There were three really big ones. One of Borneo. One of the district we were in. And one of our timber concession. Each one was ablaze with coloured pins in a pattern only Arkland knew how to decode.

He stood before the timber concession map, a 1:50,000 map the company's cartographer in the Kuala Lumpur office had drawn up. It had coloured sectors: green for unlogged areas, red for logged. The river was a wavy blue line and the roads dark-brown spokes radiating from the camp and marked over in kilometres. Arkland put his finger on Kilometre Ten.

'You stopped on the way back down. You see anything?'

So Ilpe had radioed in. Probably told Arkland the whole story, making this interview a waste of time.

'Nothing.'

Arkland made it back to his chair and slumped down again. 'We'll have to wait and see. Nothing we can do about it now. Okay,' he said with the sort of exasperated sigh form teachers use when students won't admit to stealing chalk. 'Let's get on with it.'

Ilpe and I got up and headed for the door.

'Larry,' Arkland called me back and I walked over to his desk. Ilpe got into the Land Rover and drove it to the vehicle stockade. 'When do you go on leave?'

'Monday.'

'Maybe you should hold off about this in your weekly report. Just mention the barricade. Maybe there's nothing in it.' He shrugged. 'These Penan are sturdy people. Maybe the kid's all right.'

But I knew he was dead. I knew the boy was dead. The earthslip and the thunder had told me. Hearing my father's voice confirmed it.

CHAPTER TWO

Three days later, on Sunday, I stood at the door of my rooms, looking across the timber camp. It was early and no-one was about. The sun was shining and steam rose from the red clay square that formed the centre of the camp. The men's accommodation block and the office and stores block formed one side of the square. They were low wooden buildings, each with a verandah. Opposite that block were the cookhouse and the bar. The third side was made by the vehicle stockade, a fenced-in area for the graders, the diggers, the trucks, the Cats and the Land Rovers. Opposite the stockade, the square was open to the earthen ramp that led to the road.

Sunday morning was always quiet. The Filipino men usually had an extra few beers the night before. They sang in Tagalog as they got drunk. The local Muruts we used as loggers, who hadn't trudged back to their villages, sat apart. Occasionally one of them would be overcome by alcohol and would get up to dance with the Filipino men. But usually they stayed apart, squatting on their haunches outside the cookhouse.

Arkland and I had a room each, connected to our offices, and the rest of the men shared rooms with six bunks. There were no women in the camp. No children. And for pets, some men fed the scrawny, half-wild dogs that came and went about the place, until someone took a fancy to one, and killed and cooked it.

I stood there that morning, full of the calm that comes from a good night's sleep. I had gone to bed early so I had no hangover, and for the first time since the incident I had slept without dreaming, without seeing the boy's eyes in front of me.

I began to hope that the earthslip and the thunder had been wrong, and that he was not dead.

There were hornbills high in some trees opposite me. Two

squirrels chased each other on the lower branches. Locals called the squirrel the king of the forest. That always made me smile. I was just about to go back into my room to get my binoculars when I saw the men come out of the forest behind the vehicle stockade. They came in single file and then formed a group. I estimated about fifteen. Most of them wore ragged shorts, though some had loincloths. They looked very ordinary for forest nomads. In Amazonia I had seen Indians with huge lip-plates or stunningly painted naked bodies. The Penan were small, cream-coloured, serious-looking men, their only exotic feature the large pierced earlobes some of them had. None of them carried weapons. There were no parangs, no blowpipes, no bows.

I heard a door open and Arkland stepped out of his rooms. He must have seen them coming too. He looked at me but said nothing. Though we were ten metres apart along the wooden verandah, I could see the hollows where his eyes were. He once told me he never actually slept. 'Sure, I lie down and my eyes close. But I don't actually sleep any more. I sort of hover, listening to the metal grating in my leg and the non-stop roar of airplanes somewhere over my head until the sun gets up and I can stop hovering again.'

Now he stepped off the verandah and walked towards the advancing group. I stayed on the verandah and watched as Arkland and the Penan faced each other. An old man leading the Penan group spoke in Malay and Arkland replied. He was pretty fluent, as he'd lived in Indonesia and Malaysia since Vietnam.

I knew enough to know the conversation was about the boy. '*Anak mati,*' the old man said, confirming what the earthslip and the thunder had told me. The boy was dead.

Larry's a lot older than me. Always was, you know what I mean? Ha-ha! He escaped to the Amazon after university when I was a wean. I'd love to have travelled too, but how could I with the Ma and Da getting on? Who'd bring in the coal bucket, like? And anyway, I'm not one for escaping. Not even to London, though lots of me mates are over there now. Ma said I should go. Get a job. Get

13

sorted out. What she really wanted was Larry to come back. Lawrence, she called him. He's her pet.

My brother Gerald spoke to me and I lost the conversation between Arkland and the old man. My family pressed around me, trying to protect me. But the protection they offered was stifling. First my father, now my brother. I was managing to hold my mother away, but, I wondered, for how much longer?

Raised voices brought me back to the confrontation in front of me. The old man was talking to younger men in the group, some of whom were pointing at me, anger on their faces. Then Arkland started to shout, his voice surprisingly huge for a small man. He was shouting in Malay so I couldn't understand his words, but I knew from the way he was waving his arms that he was telling them to leave.

The group of Penan men grew silent and then, in one movement, turned, formed a single file and slipped back into the forest. Arkland stood watching them and then walked back to me on the verandah.

'What did they want?' I asked.

'You.'

'Right,' I said, blowing out air.

'Well, maybe not you exactly. But the boy's dead and they want something.'

'Revenge?'

'Who knows? Justice. Revenge. Who knows?'

We stood side by side, saying nothing, looking over the square of ground in front of us. No more steam was rising and already clouds were massing behind the hills around us.

'Maybe I should cancel my leave,' I said. 'In case I'm needed.'

Arkland turned to me and smiled. 'You'll not be needed, Larry. I'll take care of it. Go on, leave like you planned.'

'But I mean, like, the police or whatever.'

'Go, Larry. Go, for Christ's sakes. It's only a dead Penan boy. The police won't give a shit. They won't even know, I'll bet. Take a vacation. Go see your mother.'

And so the next day I left the camp as planned, holding onto the thoughts that everything would be okay and that I did need to see my mother.

*****

Arkland came to see me off. We stood outside his office while Ilpe put fuel in the Land Rover. It was early morning, but already the sun was hot. Arkland was wearing a floppy hat. I was in travelling clothes. Desert boots. Light canvas trousers. A cream linen shirt. A tropical jacket lay across my brown canvas bag.

'Maybe I should take some leave? After you get back, Larry me boy.'

I knew he didn't mean it. Arkland never took leave, except a day or two at the end of a work visit to one of the company offices.

'Gets to you after a while being in camp. Know what I mean? I'll be thinking about you back in all that nice soft rain, sitting drinking good whiskey, doing a bit of whoring, only this time with white women. Yeah, maybe I will take some leave.'

He grinned foolishly at me. The small talk was meant to gloss over the death of the boy. I saw the way he wanted to play it. The ribald comments about my leave were the usual sort of banter someone in my position could expect to get. It was the ritual send-off, with no mention of work. Or crisis.

'It'll be good to see them all at home. It's been quite while,' I said.

More small talk. We shuffled our feet and I guessed we were both wishing Ilpe would get a move on. Arkland broke first.

'Where the fuck is that driver?'

'Plenty of time,' I said. 'I'm getting the afternoon train.'

Suddenly the prospect of the journey lifted my spirits. I saw myself on trains and planes, waiting in lounges, staying in hotels, having time to myself in the anonymous world of the international traveller. It would be a relief to be away from the claustrophobic world of the camp.

Then the Land Rover left the vehicle stockade and made an

elegant looping turn round the compound before coming to a halt in front of Arkland's office, facing the exit of the camp. I walked round to the passenger side and opened the door. Ilpe reached for my bag and I swung it up to him. Arkland stepped up onto the boardwalk and I stood looking at him, words tripping over themselves inside my mouth, but amounting to nothing.

Arkland shielded his eyes with his hand and shouted over the noise of the running engine.

'Get outa here, Mahon. You want I should find something urgent for you to do? Make me cancel your leave?'

I simply lowered my head and climbed into the Land Rover. No handshake. No wave. No mention of the boy or what might follow from his death. We were re-establishing our everyday patterns.

Ilpe drove us out of the camp, climbing the ramp of earth that linked us to the road I had engineered when we moved to this position. Essentially that was my job. I designed and planned the roads that led us further and further into the forest. The older stretch we turned onto now was rutted brown, compacted hard most of the time but still prone to becoming a sea of mud when the heavy rains came. Further into the forest, the road was blood red, the newly opened earth lying like a scar between the dense banks of forest.

I wanted to say something to Ilpe about the boy's death, but I couldn't find the words. An awkward silence lay between us. I had no sense that he wanted to talk to me about it. Again keeping to the old routines seemed to be what he had in mind. I looked about me, taking in the changes in the landscape; the last of the primary forest, the secondary growth, the glimpses of the sea, until finally we came to the coast and passed through our nearest little town with its houses raised on stilts along the shore, the casuarina trees, the post office, the police station and the government offices, the line of shops where Ilpe stopped for cigarettes, then on towards the railhead through the rubber plantations, the fields of palm-oil plants, the tiny hamlets and villages along the main road to the station.

For more than two hours Ilpe drove and I looked out of the window. I realised it wasn't strange that we didn't talk all that time. When we came to the station he passed me my bag as I got out of the vehicle. Something would have to be said. Something ordinary at least.

'You want to take *makan*?' Ilpe asked.

'Naw. I'll get something later. The train is leaving soon.'

Maybe I could have said something then, but Ilpe managed to be first once again. 'Have a good leave.'

Then, after a brief pause, during which he turned to face out the front window as if he was thinking about what he was going to say: 'Don't worry. Everything will be fine.'

He turned to face me and in his dark features I strived to seek the reassurance I needed.

After Ilpe left, I stood alone on the station platform, watching the train ease into position. This was the beginning of a journey home and there was no way I could avoid bringing the ghost of the boy with me.

PART TWO

Home

CHAPTER THREE

Because there are no seasons in the rainforest, there are no growth rings on the giant trees. They are ageless organisms that lived outside time until the chainsaw and the bulldozer came along. Even now, the trees I have seen on four continents seem eternal until I engineer a road to them and they are wrenched from the ground. The trees where I was born are much younger and less awesome. The last oaks are a couple of hundred years old, and stand in a public park. These are a distant echo of the great stands of oaks, ash and beech that fell finally to make the ships which England used to rule the world.

I was on the last leg of my journey home, returning from a former outpost of that great empire, where I worked for the new emperors, the people who ran the big companies. And yet as I sat in the draughty carriage, waiting at Antrim Railway Station, staring at the hedgerows full of bright yellow whin bushes blazing in the late May sunshine, my life in the international timber industry seemed like an illusion. I was more like the young man I was in 1981, over ten years before, away at college in Belfast and now on my way home, at my feet a bag full of dirty washing which my mother would receive as if it were a gift of chocolates: *Will you look at this? I don't know what you're up to in Belfast!*

And my father, ever quipping from behind the newspaper, with news of hunger-strikes in the prison and protests on the streets: *Maybe it's the zoo he's at, not the university.*

Jesus, they were so proud of me! So pleased with themselves. Look, their pride seemed to say, out of the heart of the Troubles and our honest poverty we have raised a son who is going to the Queen's University in Belfast. He is our light and our future. We are justified and made whole.

And as I left again, the bag now filled with clothes freshly washed and pressed, stepping over the remnants of the weekend's riot barricades at the corner of William Street, I was confirming the rightness of their rearing. I was the dutiful son doing them proud.

Now, with a shudder, we pulled out of the station and headed westward through the heartland of Ulster. Cullybackey, Ballymena, Ballymoney. Names known to me from pre-university myths and then rendered ordinary by the journey up and down to Belfast. And yet I remembered staying silent passing through those towns. Accents highlighted origins and it was safer to be quiet.

I looked around me now. Two old women chatted, flouncing at the bags of shopping from Belfast at their feet. A man snored, resting his head against the glass pane, bouncing there every time the train chugged over the points. An ordinary scene, holding no threats, it seemed. Yet I remained silent, not seeking to engage in conversation, staring out at the farmland and the small roads.

It was only after we had passed through Coleraine that some sense of really going home started to quicken in me. Golfers dotted the rolling sandhills, their tartan caps and gaily coloured bags marking them out against the marram-grass hillocks, beyond them an impression of the estuary and the sea. Then, at Castlerock, the first sight of rolling breakers made me sit forward in my seat.

By now I was alone in my section of the carriage. I grew impatient. I stood up to get a better view over the fences and through the gaps between the houses. I knew that I would see more as we left the tired red-brick buildings of the station and passed behind the last houses of the town, with their long thin gardens and little vegetable plots, some plastic chairs, a rockery or two, washing lines in the shape of redundant fairground carousels.

And then, suddenly, the awesome sight of the open sea lay before me as the train picked up speed. Rolling waves tumbled one behind the other, racing each other to the shore where the sand welcomed them with open and graceful quiet, soaking up their energies and their trauma. Giving them repose. On and on their ceaseless rolling went, leaving me breathless and amazed.

Then a screeching whistle blew and the train plunged into darkness, taking me completely by surprise. I fell back onto my seat, laughing to myself. How could I have forgotten the tunnels? My reflection in the blackened window showed me smiling at myself, just as I had done on the annual day trip to Portrush. We went every year. That was apart from the fortnight in the wee cabin at Lisfannon, where me and Gerald and my mother stayed all the time while my father went up and down to work some of the days. The sun always shone then. Gerald always seemed to be eating the sand. I built castles that towered over everyone else's, and I lay in the grass watching the clouds chase about the sky like a shoal of fluffy fish in an ocean of bluest blue. But my father always took one day off so we could all go to Portrush on the train.

There were special day tickets. Buckets and spades packed in net bags. Sandwiches and flasks of tea. My mother in a short-sleeved top. My father's shirtsleeves rolled up. And the highlight of the day was not the golden sands or the rush and roar of the bumper cars at Barry's Amusements, though they were wonderful. No, the highlight was going through the tunnels at Castlerock.

Gerald used to be frightened. I tried to pretend I was brave. But I couldn't remember from one year to the next when they were coming, so the shock of entering the darkness always made me giggle in excitement. Gerald sat up on my mother's lap. She held him close, whispering that we would be out soon. I stood at the glass, daring the roaring blackness to try to take me, willing myself to be brave.

Then all of a sudden you were out of it and sunlight filled the carriage once more. The view of waves and sea and headland snapped back into place. Gerald leaning forward, pointing. My mother and father smiling. And then the second one came. That was the thing about the tunnels at Castlerock.

There were two of them. That really stuck with me. Because of that you could never let your guard down for one minute.

Now, on my journey home, I was ready for the second tunnel. This time my reflection looked glummer, as if the memories of childhood were lost to me. I was old before my time, my reflection seemed to tell me. There were hollows and lines that represented the wounds and scars in my heart. It was a lived-in kind of face that looked back at me as if it had seen a ghost.

The short few minutes spent in the second tunnel stretched into an infinity of wonder and panic. Could I really be going home? Would I be able to survive it? How could I manage if they found out about the death of the boy? Should I tell them? My reflection grinned wryly. I had never really told them anything about myself. I was silent in the heartland of my own family too.

As in a cinema, the darkness exploded with an image as we came out of the tunnel. The view across to Inishowen Head, riding like a great ocean liner on the horizon, lifted my heart. The sea is still blue, I told myself. The sky looks down on you as always. Even the sun is shining and, given the rarity that is, it must be an omen.

I did my best to hold onto that lift in spirits all through the rest of the train journey along the bay, through the fertile farmland reclaimed from the sea, the sloblands of the estuary, the chemical plant and power station that marked the edge of the city, and through an arch of trees that crouched beside the river, looking across at the city climbing up the low hills. The train passed under the trees and through them I saw the slides and the swings where my mother had taken my brother and me once or twice. It was always a special trip. Across the river to Saint Columb's Park, through the barricades and the army checkpoints. An adventure. Gerald was two or three and I was twelve or thirteen. As long as no-one else was there, I could fool around with my baby brother. Otherwise, I sat sulking on a bench while my mother gently pushed Gerald, squealing delightedly, on a swing.

All of a sudden, the trees, the park and the playground were gone, and we pulled into the station. 'Londonderry' a sign said, and someone had tried to scratch out the 'London'. I smiled, and I remembered how, when I had first met Arkland, I told him the city I came from was called either Londonderry or Derry, depending on your political view.

'But what about the mailman? What does he do about it?'

'He just deals with either, I suppose. I don't really know.'

'And that's what the war is all about there? Some guys want to call it Derry and they're Catholics, and some guys want to call it Londonderry and they're Protestants, right?'

'Well, it's not quite...'

'Man, that makes Nam look like a pretty well-thought-out affair, and everyone knows how off the wall that scene was.'

In the five days since leaving the timber camp, that was the first pleasant memory I'd had of it. All along, from the camp to Kuala Lumpur, where I had stayed for a few days, and on to London, where I had taken a shuttle flight to Belfast, the eyes of the dead boy had harassed me. I saw them on the screen despite the in-flight film. I saw them on the dishes of microwave-zapped food the hostess served me. I saw them on the faces of the beautiful Malay children, three or four of them, travelling on my flight. Not even thoughts of my family could compete with that.

There was no-one waiting for me at the station. Foolishly, I was disappointed. I had written that I would arrive home around the 25th, but I hadn't said exactly when. I knew I should have phoned from London. Or even Belfast. Did I really want to come home? I wondered.

It's a shame he has to work away from home. But shur, where would he get work around here now? He's overqualified really. Specialised, like, in the forest end of it. And he loves the travelling. Like my old Uncle Harry who went to sea. Must be where Lawrence gets it from. You'll take another wee hot drop there!

My mother pouring out tea when a neighbour or relative called. My father, out on a site putting in windows or hanging doors or maybe erecting stairs, giving the balled top of the newel post a flick of the cloth neatly stuffed in the breast pocket of his blue dungarees. My brother Gerald at school or work, and me away, always away.

Seeing the baggage checks on my bags, taximen came forward but I brushed past them and headed for the bridge. I'd need a walk to locate and to prepare myself. I needed time before I actually met my family again. I walked over the bridge and looked up and down the River Foyle. Two army Land Rovers negotiated the roundabout on the city side of the bridge and came towards me, heading back to barracks. I could see the Guildhall clock and the low range of hills just across the border in Donegal. Scalp and Eskaheen. My father had taken me there as a child. We'd spotted birds, indulging one of his countless minor interests. Now I wondered what I would do at home for the two weeks I planned to stay.

By the time I reached the house in Marlborough Place, I began to regret not taking a taxi. I rang the doorbell and heard my mother coming down the hallway. The slipper-slap hadn't changed in the three years since I'd last seen her.

'Lawrence. My God. Lawrence!'

She clutched a hand to her neck and then patted her cheek.

'What a surprise. You should have rung. We could have met you at the airport. Show me your bags. Come in. Come in.'

She looked even younger than I remembered, with her hair in a neat bun, her glinting eyes, her creaseless face and the sturdy set of her small frame. I followed her into the hallway, gloomy after the brilliant spring sunlight of the street.

'Is Da home?' I asked.

'Your father? He's away out with Gerald. Something for the roof. Brackets. Something. You know your father. Always footering at something.'

The room we stood in was the living room and dining room, and it connected with the tiny scullery. My father, a carpenter, had lots of connections in the building trade, knew all the angles on government grants for house renovations, but had never built the back-kitchen extension all the neighbours had. The house still had two bedrooms and the original scullery, the only improvement being the bathroom and toilet Da had put in five years before. He countered any suggestions that extra rooms were needed with stunning logic.

'And shur, there's enough room for your mother and me. Gerald, he'll be gone out of the house in a few years anyway. Married. Or in England. And you're away long ago. What do we need to give ourselves the handlin' of getting back-kitchens put on for?'

A key turned in the front door and I heard my brother say, 'If we need another two or three I'll nip back down to McLaughlin's.'

'Aye, okay,' said my father, and then he came into the room. He was pulling plastic brackets for guttering out of a bag when he saw me.

'Larry. Heh, Larry. Now there's a surprise. And you're just in time to help fix the guttering. We could do with an engineer on the job. Look, Gerry. It's your brother.'

Gerald was pushing lengths of guttering into the hall and up the stairs. He turned and entered the room, dusted off his palms, stood beside our father and smiled at me. I was stunned by their faces. How alike they were, my father and my brother. Though short like my mother, Gerald was his father's son. Dark brooding eyes and thick black hair in a huge quiff. I have my father's gangly build, but my features and my hair are from my mother. Gerald and I were more like cousins, with some similarities, nothing definite, rather than brothers.

Gerald took the bag of brackets from my father. 'There's plenty there, for Christ's sake. Stop fussing.' Then he walked over to me and, taking me by the arm, he thrust the bag of brackets into my hand.

'And now Larry's here, he'll be only too glad to put them up for youse.'

I knew exactly what his words and ironic stare meant. I was home to the place he'd never left, to the parents he cared for after I had gone, and from whom he took all the complaints and bad times while listening to my mother 'Oh, Lawrence' this and 'Oh, Lawrence' that, and my father go on about the son who was an engineer out in Borneo.

I was home. I returned his stare and in his stare I imagined I saw the eyes of the dead Penan boy and I shivered.

CHAPTER FOUR

The next day Gerald and my father went to work. My mother, clearing up the breakfast things and seeing me gazing absentmindedly out of the window, said, 'You were always so good at the swimming. You always loved the baths down in William Street. Go you down and take a wee dip for yourself.'

It wasn't the first time swimming saved me, this time from my mother's anxious care and my fevered thoughts of the dead boy. I had taken it up at school and had suddenly found that my long legs and strong arms, which seemed to operate with vicious disregard for each other when I walked about, took on a marvellous coordination when I swam. I became a schoolboy champion and travelled in rickety minibuses all over Ireland to school and district galas. Chlorine burns in my nostrils and in my eyes even today from the hours of practice. I remember rising early for training. My father would have hot soup for me when I got home at eight o'clock. I was the only person in Derry, he said, who had lunch for breakfast. Then, if he was on a job, he would snap his own lunchbox shut and go off to work on some site or other. My mother slept on, Gerald cradled beside her in the warm dip just left by my father. I breakfasted alone, scribbling the homework I had been too tired to do the night before.

And at Queen's, when I went to university to be an engineer, swimming kept me out of politics. I should have fallen in with some group or other. Many of my contemporaries did. I joined nothing but the swimming club, and at an inter-university gala in Edinburgh, sponsored by the Searwood Corporation, I met a recruiter for the company and I joined them straight after graduating, becoming a junior engineer on a large concession they had in Amazonia.

Now the cool of the changing rooms at William Street Baths reminded me of the mornings I spent there as a teenager. And the shock of the water was a pleasure I had forgotten. After some mistiming, I finally got my rhythm into a slow crawl, and I felt the wonderful ease of doing something I had learned when I was a lot younger. There were just me and two other people in the pool, and I swam up and down, my breathing just right and my mind cleared of every thought, feeling or opinion. I managed to keep the Penan boy's eyes out of my mind for the first time in days, until the very realisation that I had, brought them back and I lost my concentration, sucked in water and had to grab for the side, spluttering and blowing.

The lifeguard snapped out of his reverie and looked over at me, but I waved to him. 'I'm okay,' my wave said. 'I'm okay. At least for now.'

When I went into the changing room, I noticed red weals on my shins. I had been feeling itchy for a few days so I wasn't surprised to see my skin had broken out in some kind of rash, blotchy red patches that started at my feet and ran up to my knees. I supposed they were brought on by the chlorine in the water. They itched like hell, yet tearing at them with my nails was the last thing I needed to do.

It's funny, but in all the years I had been in the rainforests, I had never been sick. Apart from simple colds and fevers every now and then, I had always been fit and healthy, with a boundless reserve of energy. I had never had a fall or experienced an injury at work. Amazing, I suppose, when you think that logging in the tropical rainforest must be one of the most dangerous jobs in the world. I'd seen plenty of death and injury, but I'd always managed to escape myself. But as I looked down at my reddened legs, it certainly seemed like my charmed existence had come to an end.

*****

Over the following days, it got worse. Every time I looked at them, my shins grew more and more raw. And though I knew it was the wrong thing to do, I couldn't help scratching them. I also couldn't hide the condition from my mother.

'Is there something wrong with your leg, Lawrence?' she asked with such a look of concern that I felt tiny inside and lied to her that everything was all right. Then I left the room and stood in the hallway, pressed against the wall, breathing hard and feeling sweat break out across my brow.

The soft voices of my mother and father came through the door.

'He's not one bit settled,' my mother said. 'Something's ailing him.'

'Ach, he's always been the restless type. It'll take him a few days to settle down.'

My father trying to make things easier. Always trying to protect my mother as if she was somehow a fine piece of furniture too delicate to be handled roughly, while he himself was some kind of old sideboard you could stub cigarettes out on and it wouldn't matter.

'He's not himself. You saw him scratching his legs there. Maybe he's after picking up some kind of tropical disease. I hope he's all right.'

Her voice made me see her perpetually wringing her hands in an act of worry, and my father, sitting opposite, maintaining a feigned interest in *The Derry Journal*'s stories of political stalemate and economic downturns, while creases of worry rippled his face.

It would really be my lucky day if I found I had a serious tropical disease. I could just contact Searwood to say I was medically unfit, send a doctor's certificate and convalesce my problems away. Never go back to the camp. Never see Arkland again. Forget the dead Penan boy in a welter of concern for my own wellbeing. A wry smile widened across my face at that idea. I knew I shouldn't be kidding myself. So I went upstairs to the bathroom, flushed the toilet to give myself a cover story and then returned to my parents in the living room.

The domestic scene that met me as I opened the door was so familiar I almost sobbed. My father sat in his usual chair, half-turned to the fire, with the last light of the evening coming over his shoulder as he read the football reports in the newspaper. My mother stood at the entry to the small kitchen, half in and half out of the room, never fully taking up a particular place, always seeming to be in between things and yet never very far away from the kitchen. There was a quality to the lighting of the room that reminded me of the words they had been sharing as I eavesdropped from the hallway. Something semi-dark and fearful, something solicitous and hankering. And the smells of tea things being washed up in the scullery. Soapy liquid bubbles, greasy plates, strong tea brewing for the later cup my father always had when he was nearly finished the paper. The only thing missing was Gerald. He should have been there. On the floor with toy cars, a great sheen on his thick black hair in the light of the coal fire. Or sitting at the table doing a homework he should have finished hours before, grinning up at me and winking. But he'd gone out straight after tea that day. He always seemed to have things to do.

And now I was left alone with my parents. I didn't know what to say so I just blurted out, 'I seem to have a bit of a rash on my shins. I wonder was it the water in the pool?'

'I told you I saw him scratching himself, didn't I?' my mother said to my father, crossing the room to stand in front of me, obviously waiting for me to show her. I looked into her eyes and saw concern and comfort. The skin rash was something I could tell her about.

'Ach, it's not much really,' I said, rolling up a trouser leg.

She dropped to her knees before me and let out a gasp. 'My God, look at this. His leg's nearly destroyed. And does it go up far?' she asked coyly as my father continued with the paper, though I had a definite sense that he was all ears.

'No. Just up to my shins.'

'It might be something you picked up out foreign.'

My mother slowly extended a finger towards my skin as if to feel one of the scabs, but stopped just short of touching it. 'You should go to the doctor with that, you know. Just to be on the safe side.'

'Oh, I don't think it will need that. It'll probably vanish as quickly as it appeared.'

But my father rustled the newspaper and his muffled voice came over the top of it. 'If your mother thinks you should go to the doctor with it, it'll do no harm to go to the doctor.' And he cleared his throat and rustled his paper some more, bringing his distant authority to my mother's care and concern as he always did.

Then Gerald walked in, took in the scene and ruefully asked was my mother going to kneel in prayer at the feet of her eldest son for the rest of the evening or would she like a wee hot cup of tay?

*****

The doctor I went to see was a fella who had been at university at the same time as me. I didn't really know him, but my family has always gone to that surgery. His father practised there and his son joined him after qualifying at Queen's. My shins seemed to be getting worse, and though the rash hadn't appeared anywhere else, it was lurid and bloodied, especially where I had scratched it.

'Larry Mahon,' the young Doctor O'Hara exclaimed. 'Now there's a blast from the past. Come in. Come in,' he called to me from the waiting room door, making the other people look at me with fearful expressions, worrying that if I knew the young doctor, would I be in with him extra long, socialising?

'You're away somewhere exotic, isn't that right? I hope you're not here with some mad tropical disease like green monkey fever. There's never much call for treatment in that line round here.'

I followed him into his consulting room and he waved me to a chair.

'Have a seat there and let me guess what year it was exactly we were at Queen's together. Sometime in the last century, I'd guess.'

'Early eighties. I left in eighty-four,' I said.

'That's right. I had a few more years to do after that. For God's sake, I had hair then.' And he threw his head back with a cheery guffaw. 'And then you went overseas into the timber business, isn't that right?'

The way he leaned towards me in his chair made me think that he was really interested, so I told him about my work and my travels in a way I knew made them sound far more exotic than they were. There was little in the way of drudgery or danger in the descriptions I gave of great forests and daring acts of logging, but very quickly I saw the doctor's eyes glaze over in the boredom that comes when we listen to anyone talking about themselves for any length of time. He was saved by the phone, which he answered briskly and professionally, listing off a range of drugs and doses.

'That was the Da,' he informed me when he hung up. 'Sorry about that. It's weird sometimes. Working with him, I mean. Sometimes we seem to be reading each other's mind. Weird.'

I envied him then. His comfort, his easy relationship with his father, his secure place and status in his own town. How had he managed to bring it off? Why was I still wandering the world? Did I still want to?

'God, it must be great seeing all those amazing places,' he continued with the enthusiasm of a boy scout. Easy for him to be enthusiastic about foreign places, I thought to myself unkindly. An armchair traveller with old copies of National Geographic scattered on the waiting room table.

'So what can I do for you then?' He switched easily into a light but professional tone, and when I described the rash and where it was, he asked me to take off my trousers so he could have a look. Unbuckling my belt, I bowed my head and smiled to myself as I remembered going to the bedroom that morning to find a pair of new underpants on the bed. I knew my mother had bought them for me out of fear of my being seen by the doctor with dirty pants on. I thought of the countless acts my mother performed for me. I felt an awful rush of bile slurping around the back of my tongue as I remembered the boy running out from behind his mother and her despairing lunge as he was swept under the wheels of our Land Rover.

'Just lie up on the couch there, will you?'

The doctor's back had been turned to me as he made notes on my file, so that he didn't notice my upset. By the time I had lain down and focused my eyes on the ceiling, swallowing hard to rid my throat of the bile and the chilling pictures in my head, I was fairly composed once more.

'Now then,' he muttered to himself as he stood over me gazing down at my lower legs. 'Itchy stuff that, I bet?'

I just nodded and he continued in his easy professional manner, asking about how long I'd had it, if it was anywhere else on my body, and if I had changed diet recently (which was a laugh when I compared the bush-pig-and-rice staples I ate in the rainforest with the stew and fries, spuds with everything, I ate in my mother's house).

'Have you ever had anything like this before? Did anyone else in your family have anything like this?'

I answered 'No' to both questions, and he murmured 'Fine' in the funnily dispassionate way that I imagined doctors used no matter how serious the illness before them.

'You can get up and put the trousers back on again,' he said as he moved across to his desk where he sat down and pulled a pad of prescription forms towards him. I got dressed and sat opposite him as he turned to me and explained, 'The rash you have is a form of psoriasis. Fortunately for you, pretty localised. Not really being an expert on tropical medicine, I would be guessing if I said you got it from contact with something during your work. Though that would be unlikely if you've never had it before. The red scaly papules and patches are typical of the forms of psoriasis I see often enough here. Sometimes it comes with stress. Or when some major upset happens. Nothing like that going on for you at the minute, is there?'

There was the briefest of flickering moments when it occurred to me that here would be a chance to tell all my worries. It had all the welcoming feel of a place of secular confession. The doctor as priest with his rarefied and semi-mystical knowledge, the vials and potions, the incantations in Latin and Greek of drug names and ailments. The confidentiality of it all. But even as the bile of my awful story filled my throat demanding to be told, I gulped it back down, erasing once more the memory of crunching tyres and a distraught mother, so that I easily replied, 'No. Everything's pretty normal. If you consider working in a rainforest normal, I suppose.'

He grinned at that and said, 'I'm going to give you a prescription for a cream that should clear it up in a few weeks. It's a hydrocortisone preparation that should be strong enough to do the job but will do you no harm. Just follow the directions on the tube when you get it.'

He began to write in an impenetrable medical hand as he continued, 'You should see some change within a few days. The rash should begin to respond and if you could come back, say, in a week's time, we can have another look at it. All right?'

I said my thanks as he stood with his hand on the handle of the door of his consulting room. We made polite chat about meeting for a pint, but nothing came of it. When I said I was only home for a couple of weeks, the doctor smilingly announced he was getting married.

'Aha!' he said with one finger raised in self-admonition, 'that means you won't be seeing me next week, not unless you drop off in Crete on the way back out, but I'm sure you wouldn't want to disturb a man's honeymoon. Just make an appointment to see my father and I'll make sure to have a word with him about you. All the best.'

I offered my congratulations and left. I made an appointment on the way out, but I never kept it.

*****

Going back to the doctor was one of a number of things I didn't do. I never did help fix the guttering. Gerald and my father seemed to get it done in the times I was out at the swimming baths or walking around the town. I had a route. Down to the Cathedral, then past the Baths and onto William Street. Round Waterloo Place and across the Guildhall Square. I avoided the shopping centre and usually found myself down by the river, staring into the sluggish water. I knew no-one really. Or if I knew them, they were married with kids and settled in the new developments out on the Culmore Road, and after a surprised 'Larry Mahon! I haven't seen you in years', they would run out of things to say and we would part, no impact of our shared youth evident at all.

I thought it would be like that when I met Claire McCann. We practically fell over each other outside Austins department store, and after a flurry of recognition and apologies, I agreed to go upstairs with her for a coffee. I stood behind her on the escalator and tried not to stare at the backs of her legs. She was wearing light cotton tights that reminded me of teenage years spent in guilt-ridden dreams of the girls from Thornhill Convent with their green tights and swirling skirts. When we got our coffee we were lucky enough to find one of the small tables near the big bay window that gave us a view of the Diamond and the cars going round looking for parking space. In the distance, the roofs dropped away to give us a glimpse of the river, near where it flowed under the elegant arch of the new bridge. As an engineer I admired the bridge, but the Foyle simply served to remind me of the river near the timber camp and the swollen urgent torrent it became in the rainy season.

'You look like you're miles away.' Claire's voice broke my reverie and I suppose I blushed, because she ran on in her excited way, 'Oh, I see you've managed to hold onto one of your most charming traits, Larry Mahon. You still have the loveliest blush in Derry. We used all be mad about you.'

I didn't remember it like that, but I smiled and asked her how she was.

'Grand,' she said. 'Real grand. Well, I would need to be, wouldn't I, and me getting married at the weekend.' She took a great slurp of her coffee, letting a rim of cream nestle above her lips.

'Congratulations. Who's the lucky fella then?'

'Myles O'Hara. You know him, I think. You were at Queen's at the same time as him.'

The doctor. Now I had even more reason to envy him, about to marry a woman from his own town, doing all the right things. My mother's voice rattled me as I watched Claire lick the cream from her top lip, her red tongue sweeping back and forth like a cat's, making me stir and shift in my seat.

Ach, Larry, wouldn't it be lovely if you met a nice girl and settled down? There's all them new houses going up out at Foyle Springs, and you should have no bother getting a job with your qualifications. Remember that wee girl of the McCanns you used to go about with?

I wondered what my mother would think when I told her the wee girl of the McCanns was marrying the doctor.

'I was in here buying my make-up for the big day. Not that I was ever a great lover of make-up. You'll know that.'

She smiled as she said it and that made me glad because it told me that she remembered times we had spent together when we were teenagers. Time spent discussing all sorts of amazing things. Music, love, the future. Holding hands on the sofa while babysitting in her older sister's house. I was never supposed to be there and the evenings were spent in a panic that her sister would return early from the night out with her husband.

'It seems like ages ago, Claire,' I said. 'All that time we spent together.'

'Yes. And now you're away off around the world and I'm settling down for a life as a small-town doctor's wife. Funny how things work out.'

I wasn't sure if I heard regret in her voice because she suddenly got up and said she had to dash to meet her dressmaker. Her last words as she headed for the lift were that I should come along to the 'evening do'. Lots of friends would be there.

'I'll send you the details,' she shouted, and the lift doors opened and she was swallowed up. I was left alone amid the pre-lunch bustle, with only thoughts of my family and the dead boy for company. And the river curving towards me like a sword.

CHAPTER FIVE

My mother reacted predictably enough when she learned I knew Claire McCann was going to marry the doctor. She felt it as a personal hurt, because she thought I would be upset.

'I was going to tell you, but I didn't bother. Shur it was years ago you knew her.' And then she sighed. 'Well, I suppose I should wish them all the best, though them McCanns were always a bit cold if you ask me.'

That kind of talk exasperated my father, so I wasn't surprised when he folded down the newspaper with a grunt to deliver his own opinion. It had always been like that, I felt. My mother would say one thing and then my father would have to have his say.

'Can we not just give them the good word and not be always looking to the bad? Good luck to her, I say. Her father's a decent working man and I never heard a bad word out of her mother's mouth, so they deserve a bit of fortune. And what could be better than seeing your own weans getting on in the world, after you educating them and all, and them settling down, and you maybe having the hope of seeing a few grandchildren about the place to give you something to be annoyed about?'

This long speech gave me such a shock that I dropped the knife I was using to put jam on a slice of bread. It clattered off the plate, off the edge of the table, and onto the floor, where it lay bleeding jam onto the lino. My father rustled the paper and went back to his reading. My mother turned on her heels and went back to the scullery and I bent to pick up the knife, conscious more than ever of the depth of misunderstanding that lay between us.

*****

Later that evening my mother came into the bedroom when I was putting the cream on my shins. I was sitting on the edge of the bed with my pyjama legs rolled up.

'Is the cream doing any good, do you think?'

'Hard to tell. It's early days yet.'

There was a pause and she rested her hand on my shoulder. 'Don't mind your father. He doesn't mean to be hard. And he's just happy to see you doing what you want to do.'

'It's okay,' I said, feeling the impulse rush up inside me to tell her everything about the accident and the dead boy. But I continued silently rubbing the cream on my shins. And when I'd finished, the movement I made to roll down the pyjamas bottoms made my mother lift her hand from my shoulder.

'I got the packet peas, Lawrence, the marrowfat ones. You always liked them,' my mother said.

I was polite and generous. I was calm and in a way I was happy. But I had no idea how I was going to stick the full two weeks of it.

*****

On the Saturday night, Gerald spent a long time in the bathroom. When he re-appeared, his black hair gleamed and his face was superbly shaven. I envied his good looks. And his youth. He was nearly twenty-one, fresh and handsome, obviously one the girls would go for. I imagined him in a disco bar eyeing up the crowd, girls tittering behind their raised glasses as they commented to each other about him.

'Eight outa ten? Wise up! Gerry Mahon?'

'Go on, he's lovely.'

'Aye, all right, seven then.'

And they would giggle and make eyes until Gerald and one of his mates strolled over, bought them drinks, danced with them and the beat rolled on.

Now he surprised me by asking me if I was going out. I had been steeling myself for another night in front of the TV, repressing my desire to tell my mother and father about running over the boy.

'Well, are you coming? Throw your coat on. We're only going out for a few pints. You'll let him out tonight, won't you, Ma? He's a big boy now, our Lawrence.'

So I threw on my coat and checked myself in the mirror. I was nearly thirty, but my skin was so tanned I looked older. Rugged good looks, I said to myself.

My parents sat in front of the telly watching a games programme. Da had three small bottles of stout beside him, and Ma had a glass of sherry and her knitting. I was glad I was going out.

'Good luck. See you later. We'll not be late.' I cringed as soon as I shouted it back.

Gerald grinned at me. 'Come on, big brother. They said it's okay for you to go out.' Then he kept up a constant chatter as we walked down the hill to the town. 'You must be worth a packet now, eh? Swiss bank account, secrets never divulged.'

'I'm doing all right.'

'And you're good to our mother too!' Gerald lilted in an old-wan's accent. Then he was serious. 'The money comes into the account every month. There's been no problems, in case you were wondering.'

I wasn't. I had checked with the accountant in London. But I was glad he'd told me. For an instant I saw us as two ordinary brothers going out for a few pints, as many others would do that night.

Then a soldier stepped round a corner near The Don Bar and stood in front of us.

'Gerry Mahon. Out on the beer then?'

His accent was from the Black Country. Wolverhampton perhaps. My own experience of English people had been uniformly good. I had worked in Australia with an engineer from Coventry, and really liked him. But this figure in jungle fatigues and helmet, his automatic rifle ready in front of him, startled me. Other soldiers had stopped me during my school days. I'd seen them skulking round corners, making their way in groups of four

41

and eight, some facing backwards, armed and scared. I remembered them crouched on one knee at the low wall on the corner of our street when I came home from early morning training. Not much older than me, but alien and dangerous.

'Who's this then, eh?'

Gerald said nothing. He looked straight ahead and the pulse in his temple beat visibly.

'Ah, come on, Gerry.' The soldier pronounced it *cam*. 'Introduce us to your big brother.'

'I'm Lawrence Mahon.'

'Larry Mahon, engineer, home on holidays,' said the soldier, turning to me. 'Well, have a nice time. It's good to see your little brother in better company than he's been keeping recently.'

Then he stepped away from us and walked backwards round a corner. We followed and saw him join the rest of the foot patrol, then turn and walk on, down towards the Cathedral.

'What was all that about?' I said.

'Nothing,' smiled Gerald, but the pulse in his temple was still beating furiously. He took out an immaculately folded handkerchief and dried the palms of his hands. 'Just some people who know me. He's a very popular fella, your wee brother. Didn't you know that? Wait'll you see the way the women go mad for him tonight.'

*****

It was as I had known it would be. The pub was crowded. Everyone was dressed for high summer, though it was only late May. Everyone's smile was radiant and the drinks were all the colours of the rainbow. Gerald ordered the pints of Guinness and I knew, when the pint arrived almost instantaneously, it would be bad. It was not the sort of place that took time over pulling pints of Guinness. Three young men came in as our drinks arrived.

'Here,' said Gerald. 'Here's the lads. Get yourselves tonight, boys. I'm with the brother here. This is Larry. And that's Pete, Dodds and Mickey.'

The lads all smiled at me. 'All right?' they said and ordered pints of lager.

'Put a taste a' lime in Mickey's, will ya? He's a bit down tonight,' Pete shouted.

'Fuck off,' said Mickey in a half-drawl, and they laughed and shuffled around, hiding their faces in their pint glasses as they looked around.

'Plenty a' talent in tonight,' said Dodds.

'Aye,' said Gerald and they all scanned the crowd, a little more brazenly now.

There was a small dance-floor at the far end of the bar. It seemed no larger than our scullery, but already people, mainly girls, were dancing. I couldn't see the DJ but heard his patter in between the records. The music was international disco, just as I'd heard in Bangkok, Rio or London. It added to the sense that we were in a resort somewhere, not up a narrow alley overlooked by a section of the city's medieval walls topped by an army observation post.

'Another pint?' said Gerald.

'My round,' I said and ordered five pints. I wasn't showing off. I just felt I should. I switched to Heineken, which the lads were drinking. Gerald and his mates spotted a table near the dance-floor and sat at it. I carried the pints over on a tray.

'That's my big brother home from Borneo. He's a wild man, I'm telling yeez.'

And they laughed, dipping their noses into the fresh pints and scanning the dance-floor.

'Are you all right here? Do you want to move on after this one?' Gerald said to me.

'No, no, this is fine. I'm fine here.'

I smiled at him and he smiled back, so I knew he was glad I was with him. I couldn't shake off the feeling that he was my son, not my brother. He seemed so young.

There were girls at the next table to us and soon members of both groups were dancing together. Another round of pints appeared, and Gerald and his mates came and went from the table, as the music got louder, the crowd got bigger and the beat rolled on.

Alcohol makes me grow quieter. I don't get any lift before its real effect, depression, hits. I go into a glazed melancholy that is pleasant enough but often unnerving for people around me. The lads didn't mind and Gerald just checked with me every now and then. I kept assuring him I was fine as I drifted further and further away from the bar, the disco and the people.

Thoughts of work wandered in and out of my head. Some trucks were being repaired when I left. Were they back on the road yet? They would need to be. But that's Arkland's problem, let him deal with it. The Penan. Had they come back again, looking for me? The police. I kept worrying about the police. All week I had worried about the police. The alcohol had loosened my grip and I couldn't push the thoughts away.

'Are you not dancing?'

Dodds's face was flushed and sweaty. It had red blotches where shaving had been too much for his fair skin. 'Some talent here tonight,' he said with a slight slur. Then he added, 'You're an engineer, aren't you?' I nodded. 'Me too,' he continued. 'Well, a mechanic like. I'm doing classes at the Tech. Then I'm going to get outa this fucking place. I don't mean the bar just.' He laughed. 'I mean the town. This town. There's nothing in it.'

I nodded as Dodds got up to return to the dance-floor, but I couldn't form words. It must have been the alcohol. Tears started to well up in my eyes and roll down my cheeks. I hadn't really managed to shake off thoughts of the boy killed in the rainforest.

*****

The next day I bought every Sunday paper at the shop. Then I scanned them all in silence while my mother and father went to Mass. There was no talk of me going. That had been dealt with a long time ago. I guessed my mother prayed for me to come back into the fold. I was just glad she didn't harangue me or make me feel guilty.

There was no news of Borneo in the Sunday papers, not even in the business sections of the quality press. Nothing about a boy being killed, or police investigations. Nothing about me or Arkland or the company. I searched the papers for reassurance, even though I knew that just because it wasn't in the papers didn't mean things weren't unravelling at the camp.

'Anything in that pile of papers about the match?' my father said when he came in. He lifted one and turned to the sports sections. 'If we win today we'll go clear at the top of the table.'

Then Gerald came down in his pyjamas, yawning and scratching his belly.

'What about Mass, Gerald?' said my mother from the kitchen.

'I got it last night,' he shouted, winking at me.

She brought his breakfast in on a tray and I pushed the papers aside to let her put it down. 'Any jobs for you here, Lawrence? Or in London even?'

It was a constant theme for her. She wanted me to come back home, to live and work nearby. Now it seemed like a good idea.

'Ah, he doesn't want to come back here, Ma,' said Gerald. 'You should have seen the women going mad for him last night when they heard he worked in Borneo. He could have had his pick of twenty.'

'I'm sure Lawrence has more sense,' said mother.

And Gerald winked at me again. I smiled back, remembering that I'd come home alone while he and the lads had gone on somewhere with the women from the next table. I had heard the stairs creak as he tiptoed to bed. It had been nearly morning and my bladder had been full of Heineken and my mind full of the Penan boy's face.

Gerald went to get dressed and didn't come down again until Sunday lunch was on the table. He began to eat as if he hadn't seen food for days. There was pork steak, peas, roast and boiled potatoes, and apple sauce. Then there was stewed apple and custard, tart and sweet at the same time, just like I remembered it from childhood.

I washed up afterwards, running the soap suds over the plates in such a preoccupied way that my mother asked, 'Is something bothering you, Lawrence? Is that cream not doing the rash any good?'

'No, no. It's nothing. Nothing at all,' I lied. I knew that hurt her. I turned to her but I couldn't bring myself to confide in her.

Later I was sitting in an armchair leafing through the Sunday papers again. There had to be some news from Borneo in them.

'Are you not going to the match with your father then?' my mother called from the kitchen.

'No.'

My father and Gerald came into the room. They wore red and white scarves, and my father had a large flask in his coat pocket.

'Right. We're off. What about you, Larry? You sure you don't want to come?'

'No thanks,' I said. 'I might go out for a walk in a wee while.' My native tongue was coming back. I heard them go down the hall, muttering the latest team news. The front door slammed as my mother came into the room.

'You're not away with them then?'

'No.'

'Did I hear you saying you were going for a walk?'

I'd only said it to put my father off. I didn't intend going anywhere. But when I saw the excitement in my mother's face I said, 'Yes, that's right. Do you want to come?'

She patted her bun and smoothed her skirt. 'Just give me a minute to get ready. Just a minute.'

It was like the walks on Sundays many years before. Gerald in the pram. Me by her side. 'Mystery Tours' she called them. We would go out straight after Sunday dinner and follow different ways, always different it seemed to me, my mother keeping up a constant chatter about people's gardens, window boxes and other features of our city. She told me about the Walls and the Siege, making me run my fingers along the stones. She told me about St Columba, and when we passed his sacred well

46

she would tell me of his travels in Donegal and to Iona. And she told me about the oaks that had once covered all the hills around Derry, and how they were the reason St Columba had made a settlement there and kept the pagans' name for it.

'Do you fancy going out as far as St Columb's Park?' I said.

'Aye. That'd be great. I haven't been over there in years.'

She was like a girl on a spree. We crossed Craigavon Bridge and followed the new road out past Ebrington Barracks. Two Land Rovers were parked back to back on the pavement as policemen checked cars. We had to walk out onto the road to get around them. And then we went into the park.

We immediately chose the route over the little bridge, down through the tall trees shading the wall beside the hospital and the barracks. Then out of the trees and onto the open ground and the rolling grassy slopes, where I had always raced on and clambered to the top of a mound and spun round to see my mother pushing Gerald. And I would wave to her and shout, 'I am up here in the clouds. Yeez look wile wee down there.'

These memories almost made me break from my mother as we left the trees. She had slipped her arm through mine and grinned up at me as she did so, just as we passed the Land Rovers. Protect me, she seemed to be saying, I'm getting old.

'It's years since I was here. Must have been when you were boys, you and Gerald. Hasn't changed much, has it?'

It hadn't. The lush grass rolled over the slopes as it had in my boyhood and I smelled its freshness just as if I was pressing my face against it like I did when I was a boy. We walked up and over a small hill, and two boys on bikes raced past us. I envied them their youth and their innocence as they laughed together, attempting wheelies.

We walked on and re-entered the trees. Oaks, with new leaves growing, stood around us. I slipped my mother's arm out of mine and ignored her enquiring glance. I walked over to one of the trees and ran my fingers over the rough bark.

'There are trees in the world that have edible bark, you know.'

My mother smiled. She liked me showing off my knowledge. 'Where?' she asked.

'Papua New Guinea, Amazonia. Quite a few of them.'

'Any near where you are now?'

'I don't know. Maybe. No-one at the camp knows. Not interested, I suppose. The Penan know, I imagine. They're the people who live by wandering in the forest. There's a lot of them where I am now. I suppose they would know.'

I patted the tree and looked up at the branches. Two to three hundred years old, I guessed. Nothing compared to trees I'd seen.

My mother moved closer to me as the two boys came racing back on their bikes. Their tyres crunched the gravel path, and when they passed by the tree where we stood, one of them, a redhead with a top tooth missing from his smile, tried a wheelie. He leaned right back, pulling hard on the handlebars. His front wheel left the ground and the back one slewed and slithered on the gravel until he keeled over onto the path. My mother and I went to him immediately.

'Are you okay?' I said.

'Yeah,' he said. 'Okay.'

I helped him up and pulled his bike to one side. It wasn't damaged. I saw some blood on his knee. 'You'd better go home and get that washed,' I said.

He looked down at his knee and then back up at me. 'It's nothing. Thanks,' he said, smiling.

I saw the gap in his smile and the freckles on his nose. Then my heart seemed to stop in my chest as the boy's face was transformed until it was the Penan boy in front of me smiling and saying, 'It's nothing. Thanks.'

Then his friend came back to him and they both got back on their bikes and cycled off, laughing as they had before.

'Are you all right, Lawrence?' my mother asked quietly. I couldn't tell her that it felt like my heart had stopped. How could I tell her I had seen a ghost?

'It's all right, Ma. Stood up too quickly after helping the wee boy, that's all.' There was a bench near us and she led me to it.

When I sat down I was looking back at the clump of oaks, and for an awful moment they seemed to grow suddenly upwards with great lianas dangling from them and great buttresses flanking them. Then the spasm passed and the park returned to normal again. Family groups out for a Sunday afternoon stroll. Elderly men in Barbour jackets walking dogs on leashes.

'Must have been something I ate,' I said, and I knew immediately how stupid that was. It would only make my mother's worries worse. She looked at me, creases lining her forehead and her neat bun pert on her head. I wanted to tell her then. I wanted to let it all go, but I swallowed it back and repeated that I was all right, and to prove it I got up and said we should get a move on if we wanted to see all around the park and get home before Da and Gerald got back.

We looked like any of the other people in the park that afternoon. A mother and her son out enjoying the spring weather. But if you looked closely you'd have seen the worried look on the mother's face and the leaden eyes of the son.

CHAPTER SIX

I began my second week's leave frantic to get back to Borneo. I couldn't bear not knowing what was happening out there. I phoned the London office on a pretext, but in the course of a general chat about things they said they had received no news from the camp. Just routine reports. Nothing special.

My mother was keeping a watchful eye on me, offering me special foods, and suggesting I got more sleep. 'Is anything bothering you?' she asked.

'No, nothing,' I said and left for the swimming baths. It was the only thing I could fill my time with, and the irony of this struck me as I remembered how important swimming had been to me as a teenager.

The evenings were the worst. I struggled through with TV viewing and reading on Sunday and Monday evenings, then on Tuesday morning I went for a walk and got soaked in a spring shower that followed me all the way back from Sheriff's Mountain, just outside the city.

Gerald sensed my unease and said to me, 'You're fed up here, aren't you? You want to go back out there this minute, don't you?'

I nodded. I couldn't lie to him.

'Well, look, try to stick it out till next week. If not for Ma and Da's sakes, then for mine, because when you leave I'll have to keep them smiling, and if you leave early it'll be worse for me because Ma will think there's something up with you and Da will be all guilty again because he thinks he did something to drive you away. So stay till next week like you planned. Right? For my sake.'

As things turned out, I was glad I stayed for Gerald's sake. I even managed to perk up a little and even if I couldn't stop worrying about what was happening out at the camp and really wanting to be out there, I made a better job of hiding it.

*****

Then a short note in Claire's delicate scrawl came, telling me that I must come to the 'evening do'. Lots of old friends would be there. She'd signed it 'See you there, Claire and Myles', but I wasn't really sure that he would want me along. Old boyfriend and all. I saw her persuading him, saying it would do no harm. It had all been years ago.

Of course my mother fastened onto this note as a matter of great importance. Whatever she might have thought about my missed opportunity or Claire's failure to realise my worth, I would have to be sorted out properly for this wedding. That meant a present and a suit. When I said that I was only going to the party in the evening, that what I had received did not amount to a 'full' invitation and so there was no need for a wedding present as such, she would have none of it. And I would have to buy a new suit. Something navy blue. My best colour, she said. My father really enjoyed my discomfiture in the face of all this attention.

'Shur I have that pinstriped one in the wardrobe I haven't worn for years. He could get that dry-cleaned and he'll be grand.'

He smiled at me, winking behind my mother's back, seeking to draw me into his own pattern of, as he called it, 'humouring' her. Gerald got in on the act too.

'You know that song, Ma. The one about going to a wedding leading to another. Maybe Lawrence will get lucky with one of the bridesmaids.'

'Stop your noise, you. You're worse than your father,' my mother admonished him, but you could tell she secretly hoped there was some truth in the words of the song.

*****

I came upon my mother the next morning taking great bath towels out of an Austins bag and laying them across the table in the living room.

'You don't have to give these if you don't like them. If you don't think it's a good idea. I kept the receipt.' She pulled and flounced the heavy royal-blue material, inviting me to touch them. I placed my hands among the folds and felt their wonderful softness.

'They're very good quality. A bit pricey, but I thought it best. And as I said, if you don't like them they'll take them back.'

I took the hefty cloth in my arms and felt their weight and their softness overwhelm me. Words stuck in my throat but I managed to rasp out, 'Thanks, Ma. These are fine. Brilliant.'

And even that rasping thanks seemed to hearten her, because laughter and then bright tears started to glisten in her eyes so that I just managed to get out of the room before she could ask what was upsetting me.

I parcelled the towels later in paper that my mother had also brought home. She'd even bought a card, and I signed my name to it with best wishes. The pretty bouquets and tiny horseshoes on the paper had made my mother go all moony. They just made me feel confused and uneasy. Should this have been me?

My mother's opinion was that I should take the parcel up to the McCann house and pay my respects, but when I refused, and she saw the look in my eye, she decided to let it go. Gerald came to the rescue, saying he was going up that way anyway and that he would hand it into the house. He had the parcel whisked up, the card tucked into the folds of the paper, and was out of the house before my mother could raise an objection.

She preened and picked a bit at the suit I finally bought. 'The lapels are narrow, aren't they? I don't know, but I think double-breasted would have been better.' But overall she was happy enough, and even allowed that, with a bit of a polishing and shining, the black shoes I had would be all right. She bought me some new socks to go with the pants she had bought me earlier, and we had a dress-rehearsal night before the wedding itself, mainly at Gerald's insistence.

'Look, Lawrence,' he said to me up in the bedroom as I finished dressing, 'if it gives them bit of crack, where's the harm in it? We all know we're playing a game, as if it was your wedding this whole drama was about. So play your part like a good leading man and get downstairs for the photocall.'

I knew he was right, but I hadn't the nerve to tell him that it was all right for him to think it was a good laugh, he wasn't playing the part of the dupe. But instead I smiled at him, gave him a look and said, 'What do you think?'

He gave me a thumbs up and mouthed 'Dead on!' before leading me down the stairs to where our parents were waiting. My mother just managed to hold back her tears when she saw me. My father made a crack about his own pinstriped suit at least having two rows of buttons, and Gerald ran about saying mad things in a whole variety of funny voices.

'Ach, shur he has the girls' hearts broke, that Mahon fella. Isn't he a credit to his mother all the same, and the electrification he got up at the university?'

Then, in his own voice, he shepherded us all away from the fireplace with big gestures of his hands, and producing a camera from the top of the telly, he made us line up.

'But I can't have me photo taken like this,' squealed my mother.

'Just take your apron off, woman,' my father advised, laying aside his newspaper for once and sticking his shoulders back like a sentry. I stood between them like a condemned man and Gerald took the photo. Then, with heightening hilarity, he piled books and cushions on top of the table, balanced the camera on them, pressed the timer button and rushed across to join us.

'Just hold it there, folks. One for the family album.'

'You'll get nothing but the tops of our heads the way that thing is pointed.'

My father had to have an opinion on everything and then the camera flashed brightly and we all burst out laughing. I treasure the print that came from that hilarious photo. The four of us in a line, Gerald squeezed in next to me at my elbow, looking up with a knowing grin. My father finishing a sentence. My mother looking amazed.

*****

The wedding itself turned out to be a minor, if farcical, mistake for me. I spent the whole evening feeling I was in the wrong place and yet stuck to the ground by some sort of paralysis that made it impossible for me to slip away quietly even though my head was telling me that was the right thing to do.

Part of the problem was that the 'do' was held in a country house hotel and restaurant outside the city so I just couldn't walk away. Getting a taxi would have drawn attention to myself. And I suppose I have to admit a certain fascination with the whole event. Morbid in its own way. Could that have been me, the flushed and ebullient groom, his mates pawing around him, laughing too loud, drunk on wine and brandy after the big meal?

To give him credit, Myles did come to me when he saw me enter the function room. 'Thanks for coming, Larry. It's getting a bit mad but have a few quick blasts to catch up and then we'll go into the dancing. The bar's free here but not in there I'm afraid.'

Then he led me to the bar and called a Black Bush for me. We clinked glasses in the fashion of old adversaries making up for something and he whirled off, muttering about seeing to the band.

I leaned against the bar and surveyed the room. Jesus, this is a riot, I thought. I gulped on the whiskey and tried to separate his family from Claire's. That group in the corner, women of all ages in gaily coloured dresses, some still wearing hats, looked like Claire's mother, aunt and sisters. The McCanns. Then I saw the doctor, Mr O'Hara senior, in earnest conversation with another man I took to be a family friend. I imagined them talking about golf or fishing, happy in their later years to see their families around them growing into the comforts they had enjoyed. Happy to know their families were moving on in similar ways. I needed another gulp on the whiskey to stifle the guilt rising in me because I couldn't bring all that off for my parents.

Ach, I don't know if he'll ever marry, our Lawrence. Not that he's not had plenty of chances. That wee girl of the McCanns was mad about him. And that's just one. Long as he doesn't get married out there and bring us back a surprise.

My mother's voice, a false laugh in it. I pictured her teasing out her fears and hopes in conversation with Mrs Heaney, a neighbour. I shivered and the voice and the picture vanished.

I needed more whiskey. I waved to the barman, who gave me a generous double with a 'Get that into you now' smile.

When I turned round again, Claire was beside me, a mass of shimmering white material laid out to show off her beautiful shoulders and the way her auburn hair fell upon them. I must have blushed because she said, 'See, Larry Mahon. You've never lost it. Best reddner in Derry.'

Her smile lit her face and I said, 'You look brilliant.'

'Thanks. Everyone's been great. And the towels were lovely, by the way. Lovely.'

She wasn't being polite. I could see that. 'My mother picked them out,' I said.

'Ach, she's very good to you, isn't she?' she quipped, but I knew she wasn't being hard on me. It was a fairly standard jibe.

A bridesmaid in a full blue dress came up and grabbed Claire by the arm, saying, 'They want you in the other room to start the dancing. Come on.'

Then she caught sight of me and gasped, 'Larry Mahon, I haven't seen you in a million years.'

I vaguely recognised her, but before I could speak she laughed and turned away. Claire followed her with a cheerful shrug. I couldn't remember who the bridesmaid was. Some friend of Claire's from school, I supposed.

That's the way it seemed to be with everyone. I seemed to be able to recognise the older people, but have trouble pinning down the people my own age. Not that I got to talk to many of them. Everyone seemed to be in couples and family groups. Even the gang of fellas who were Myles's buddies kept homing back to tables where women I took to be their wives maintained bases.

The crowd was moving into a bigger room for the dancing and in an ormolu mirror in the lobby I caught a glimpse of myself as I followed them. Not bad, I thought to myself. Bit of a tan. Looks good in the blue suit. Hair okay. Enough of it anyway. Eligible bachelor? Perhaps.

Then my eyes refocused to take in the luxurious plant that rose behind me in the reflection, and I saw myself cowed by greenery, surrounded by great trees, immersed in layers of vegetation, smothered by forests of my own uncertainties and weaknesses so that I had an awful feeling of not really knowing what I was doing there.

The empty sense of being lost deepened as the evening wore on. It wasn't very clear where I should sit, as I wasn't with any party as such, so I found myself at a stool beside the hatch that served as a bar.

I could see everything from there. The four-piece band that did an excellent job of getting everyone out dancing, with old favourites and rock-and-roll hits. The efforts made by relatives to ask people from the other family to dance. The young priest with his collar askew, talking earnestly to the bridesmaid in blue. Myles dancing with Claire's mother. Claire dancing with the senior doctor.

It was all making me feel uneasy, and my shins started to itch furiously so that I found myself in the unhappy situation of having a trouser leg halfway up as I scratched at the red weals – should have put more of that blasted cream on, I was thinking to myself – when I heard a voice say, 'Nice tan.'

I looked up to see the bridesmaid in the blue dress grinning down at my leg. 'You can even see it in your face under the blush,' she said. 'Claire told me about that.' Then she turned her head to one side and said, 'You don't remember me, do you?'

When I shook my head, still bent over pulling the trouser leg down over the sock again, she continued, 'I'm Bronagh, Claire's sister.'

Then I remembered a much younger girl who used to giggle and squirm in delight to tease Claire whenever she and her friends came upon us out somewhere. In Brooke Park. In the Lep having a coffee, all A-Level cool.

'You fancy a drink?'

She was like Claire, but stronger almost. Made me think of me and Gerald. He was younger than me, but much more wise. Is that because he and Bronagh had grown up some years later than myself and Claire? They had grown up right through it. Is that what it meant to be war babies? Me and Claire were nearly adolescents when the Troubles started. Or maybe it just affected us all differently, each in our own way.

'Thanks,' I said and lifted my glass to the waiting barman, who put another Black Bush into it. 'It's always safer to stay with the same drink.' It seemed as if Bronagh felt the same.

'Red wine for me. Best not to mix it at this stage.'

We clinked glasses and had an awkward moment or two looking round the room. She was first to manage to come up with something to say.

'Claire tells me you work in a rainforest somewhere.'

'That's right. In Borneo.'

'Wow!' It was only semi-mocking. I could tell from her eyes. 'You're home on holidays then?'

'Yes. Staying with me Ma and Da.'

'Ah, the Ma and Da. Getting a bit of good grub and your Ma catching up on all your dirty washing.'

'Not exactly.'

She had the same sense of fun as her sister, but with more irony in it. I found I was enjoying myself.

'They must be very proud of you. Such an exotic creature to have as a son.'

I checked her eyes, a lighter blue than her dress, but there was no mocking in them. I paused before saying, 'I think they are proud all right. A wee bit. But I think they're also confused and disappointed. Sometimes I feel I've let them down.'

I hadn't meant to get so serious. Bronagh picked up my

change of tone and put her glass down on the bar.

'How do you mean?'

'I don't know. Something about this, I suppose,' I said, gesturing with my glass at the wedding reception. 'I think they'd have preferred me to have settled down and have a job in the town.'

'With someone like Claire?'

I must have blushed again because she continued, 'Doesn't take much to give you a reddner, Larry Mahon. It's kind of cute, in a boy scout sort of a way. Go on. Don't pretend that you and Claire weren't the twosome of the year when you were at school.'

'That was years ago.'

My face seemed to be burning off me but I was saved by the band leader, a stout fellow in a black suit and a fleecy white shirt showing a mat of chest hair in which nestled a star-sign medallion.

'Come on, everybody. Let's do the *Hokey Cokey*.'

A cheer went up and there was a jovial rush and push between tables onto the tiny dance space.

'Come on, Larry Mahon. Drink up. This is what getting married is really about.'

She took my hand and led me onto the floor where a circle had been formed. Already, people were putting their left hand in, putting their left hand out, doing the *Hokey Cokey* and shaking all about. I surprised myself by getting into it really fast, pinned between Bronagh and the young priest who kept leering across at her. Then we did the *Hucklebuck*, and I felt the sweat on my forehead as I moved and bounced, hands in the air, laughing to myself at the line 'If you don't know how to do it, ask your little sis.'

'Keep it going,' shouted the bandleader. 'Shur yeez are only warming up.' His announcement that we were ready for *The Birdy Song* was greeted with mock groans. But nobody left the dance-floor. The circle seemed to get bigger. I was the only man with a jacket still on and I took it off and hung it over a chair behind me as we went into the routine of familiar movements. I couldn't guess how I knew how to do this. Tweaking my fingers, flapping my elbows, shaking my hips.

It was the most natural thing in the world for me to be

sitting with Claire's extended family at the end of the dance set. A sprawl of tables and chairs, occupied by brothers, sisters, aunts and uncles, centred on her parents. I had found a chair at the extreme edge of the group when Bronagh sat next to me. She had brought fresh drinks from the bar hatch.

'Now they're really married,' she said, catching her breath. 'That's the rubber stamp on it. Properly. All that stuff with the priest in the Cathedral was simply a prelude to this ritual here. Doing *The Birdy Song* sealed it. They're hitched now.'

She held up her glass and I clinked it with mine and grinned in agreement. 'Do you live in Derry still?' I asked her.

'No. London mostly. Work takes me all over the place.'

'What do you do?'

'I work as a film editor, freelance most of the time, though I have a couple of semi-permanent contracts.'

'Pretty exotic yourself, aren't you?'

She smiled back at me and I had a feeling of comfort that I rarely experienced talking to women. I looked at her and knew that she was very like Claire but also very different. I was amazed at how much like Gerald and me that made them, though I didn't think she was as young as Gerald.

'When do you go back to London? Or wherever?'

'Couple of days. And you?'

'End of the week. I don't know really. Maybe next week.' My old sense of incompetence and awkwardness welled up in me.

Just say you'll meet her for lunch before she goes back. Just ask her if she'd like to go for a drink.

Voices in my head. My own and then my father's.

Look, Larry. Do it for your mother's sake. It's not a big thing is it? Just to make her happy? She only wants what's best for you, you know. Stop avoiding things.

Bronagh's voice brought me back to reality. 'What exactly do you do in the rainforest?'

'I work for a timber company. Logging hardwood. I'm the surveyor, engineer and general technical dogsbody.'

There was more bitterness in my answer than I realised I

had in me. And I suppose it was the quizzical look in her eyes, the swirl of good whiskey inside my belly, the heat and noise of the wedding 'do' that made me drop my guard.

'It's okay most of the time. It's just that an awful thing happened before I came away. A boy was killed. A Penan boy.' I stumbled to continue. 'We knocked… I was in a Land Rover that knocked him down. I can't get his face out of my head.'

I had turned away from her, as if I was speaking to myself. I felt her hand on my shirtsleeve and turned back to see her warm look. It made the tears well forward in my eyes, globules of liquid sitting on my lids. It was a delicious moment of release and comfort that must surely have offered more, but all in a rush, people about us started to get out of their chairs and make for the dance space.

A voice beside me shouted, 'Come on, Bronagh, time to give your sister the big send-off.'

Bodies got between us and I saw her swept off her seat and into the tide of family and friends. She tugged at my shirtsleeve, but I was immobile and the press of people broke her grip. The music started again and a great circle formed. Apart from a few elderly aunts and a very drunken man lying asleep across a table, I was the only one not dancing.

I had an awful sense of having made a mistake. I got up and retrieved my jacket from a nearby chair and left the hotel quietly. No-one saw me, and I convinced myself I had made the right move when I merged with a group of late-night revellers returning from a night in the town and managed to catch the taxi they had come in before it sped back to the city.

All the way home I sat in the back watching the city flash by, and I tried to hold onto the real meaning of what I'd done, advising myself that this was not a good time to get involved with someone. Images of my face in the darkened window of the train as it passed through the tunnels at Castlerock came to me. Two of them, the images said. Always two of them. Don't get caught by the second one. Be careful. Always careful.

CHAPTER SEVEN

On Friday night I went to a pub quiz with Gerald. His friends were there and we formed a team. Each team sat at a table and was given an answer sheet. The quizmaster read out rounds of questions and after each round the answer sheet was collected and a new one handed out. It was noisy and boisterous. People called answers and remarks. It wasn't too serious, and there were special questions in between rounds with free pints for prizes. Everyone enjoyed it as far as I could make out.

Gerald's friends kept expecting me to know the answers. It made me feel like I was back at Queen's where I fell into discussions with peers of mine who had gone political. I remembered being tongue-tied and angry at not being able to keep up in those conversations. In the end, I used to laugh and say, 'Heh, I'm an engineer. What do I know about politics?' The quiz made me feel like that, because it showed how little I knew about history, politics and current events. I became really uncomfortable in the group at the table.

'Jesus, weren't you at university? Ah, come on, you must know that one.'

But I didn't. I hardly knew any of them. And any answers I did give were invariably wrong. I began to drift out of the quiz. I sat back in my chair while the others hunched over the table and the answer sheet, screwed their faces up in concentration and shouted remarks at friends around them.

Eventually I left the table, went to buy a round and just stayed at the bar, looking at my reflection in the mirrors and slowly sipping my pint.

'Bout ye, Larry Mahon. Long time no see, kid.'

I turned to the man who had just come to the bar beside me. He was smiling at me, but I didn't recognise him. Then a barman

61

came and he turned round saying, 'Two Smithwicks, a vodka and Coke and a Tia Maria with ice.' He was taller than me and his scrawny neck stuck out from his shirt collar. He had jet-black hair swept back off his forehead, and when he turned back to me still smiling, I saw his sharp brown eyes and fine nose.

'So, what about ya? Still in the jungles is it? Last I heard, you were for Brazil or some place?'

Then I recognised him, but I still couldn't get the name. 'Yeah, that's me, still in the jungles,' I said.

'You here with the brother, Gerry?'

'Yeah. He's over there. And you, what are you doing now? I haven't seen you since Queen's.'

'Must be,' he agreed. Then the barman came back with his drinks and he handed over the money, collected his change and said, 'Better get back before the last round starts. Watch them two pints while I take these over first.'

I still couldn't get his name. And when he came back for his pints he just said, 'Enjoy yourself. Might see you before you head off again. Right?'

'Right,' I said. I remembered him then. I was at Queen's with him, but he did History and got involved in the Students' Union. He'd try to persuade me to be more active. I remember telling him I was active enough with the swimming club.

The quizmaster announced the last question and then collected the answer sheets. The noise level rose even more and the bar became crowded as the quiz broke up. Gerald came up to me. 'You all right?' he said.

'Yeah. Fine. Just… Well, the quiz is not my scene.'

'It's only a bit of a laugh.'

'I know. I just… I'm no good at them, that's all.'

'Maybe if the questions had been engineering or forest ones, you'd have been happier.'

'Maybe.'

'You don't know much about our history, do you?' He asked it innocently enough, but I felt suddenly angry.

'What do you mean "our" history, and why the hell should

I want to know anything about it?'

'Take it easy,' he said. 'I saw you talking to Mick Gallagher.'

'Yeah. I couldn't remember his name. I haven't seen him for years.'

'He was inside.'

'And now. What's he doing now?'

'He's on the city council. Got elected last year. We have five councillors now, but why the hell would you want to know anything about that? It never made the Borneo newspapers.'

It was as if I had suddenly woken up to something. As if I had suddenly come to. I looked around the pub at the smiling faces and the quizmaster about to announce the winning table.

'What's this quiz for? Who's running it? What's the money on the door for?' I asked.

'It's for a drama group. Ex-prisoners and their families. They need money.'

'Republican prisoners?'

'Yeah. They're putting on a play about life inside.'

I turned right round to face my brother. It struck me again how like my father he was. The same strong good looks, the same twinkling eyes.

'Are you involved?' I said.

'Ach, Larry, wise up...'

'Are you?' I was almost shouting. 'Do Ma and Da know you're involved? Do they?'

But his answer was drowned by the roar of the crowd as the winners were announced, and Dodds came up to us.

'Jesus, we're after winning. For fuck's sake, we won the bottle of whiskey!'

And he dragged Gerald across the floor to the quizmaster's table where Mickey and Pete were already waiting. Gerald received the bottle of whiskey and was escorted by his friends back to their table. Then Dodds came to the bar again.

'Jesus, fucking brilliant. That brother of yours is brilliant. He really knows his stuff. Tommy, Tommy. Go on, give us four wee glasses, will ya? No, give us five.'

63

As the barman handed him the whiskey glasses, Dodds said to me, 'Come on back to the table, Larry boy. It's celebration time.'

And he clinked the glasses together and began a chorus of 'Here we go, here we go, here we go', which was taken up by his friends at the table. I followed him and pulled up a stool again as a DJ started sound-checking his system.

Gerald poured out the whiskey. Everyone at our table got a full glass, and friends all round got some too. The DJ played the first record, a soul hit from the sixties, and turned on the disco lights. I sipped at the whiskey and watched my brother. He caught my eye and raised his glass in salute and winked. Then he mouthed '*Tiochfaidh ár lá*', but I couldn't be sure that he wasn't just mocking me.

By the end of the night, Mickey and Dodds were falling-down drunk. Pete wasn't too bad, and he and Gerald persuaded them not to go for chips and loaded them into a taxi. Pete travelled with them, and Gerald and I set off to walk home.

The night was clear and cold. Though it was May, it felt as if there would be frost by morning. My breath blew clouds in front of my face and I was amazed at how drunk I was. I was deeply morose, huddled into myself.

Gerald and I walked home in silence. He was steady on his feet while I meandered about. 'You're not drunk?' I said as we reached the house.

'I don't drink much really. It's a mug's game.' He slotted the key into the lock first go, and as he opened the door he said to me, 'You don't have to worry about me. I'll be all right.'

Then I followed him up the stairs. He made it soundlessly. I touched every creaking step.

*****

Gerald was beside me in the Land Rover. I was driving and couldn't keep it on the road. It was a quagmire, mid-monsoon season. The wipers swished vainly at the rain and Gerald turned to me, saying, 'Will you be all right? Can you manage it? Will

I be all right?' The Land Rover slewed across the road in the mud, almost to the edge of the road. I caught a glimpse of a forest-filled ravine miles below and I clenched my hands onto the steering wheel, but it was too late as we went over and down, hurtling through space. I kept speaking to Gerald.

'You'll be all right. Yes, you'll be all right.'

I sat bolt upright in bed as the front door slammed open. Heavy boots crashed up the stairs and the bedroom door was flung open so hard the receiver for the lock flew off the jamb. The light was switched on, and an awful screaming began as my mother hurried onto the small landing between the bedrooms. I could see her trying to push past the soldiers who filled the doorway to the bedroom I shared with Gerald. An RUC man came into the room and shouted at the top of his voice, trying to overcome my mother's screams.

'Gerald Mahon. Put on some clothes and come with us.'

I struggled to shake off sleep. I was sweating from the dream, and the chill of the morning made me shiver. I saw Gerald pull on some trousers and a sweater.

'It's okay, Ma,' he said in a quiet but firm voice, and as my mother's screaming stopped, an eerie silence filled the house.

'What's going on here?' I said.

'Who's this?' the RUC man said.

'It's the older brother home on holidays.' The soldier beside him answered, before turning to me. 'You think you'd have taken better care of your young brother here than letting him get mixed up with bad boys then, wouldn't ya?'

I remembered the Black Country accent from the street a few days before.

The RUC man said, 'Come on,' and Gerald was led down the stairs. It was only then that I saw my father. He was wearing pyjama tops and bottoms that didn't match, and he held the lock receiver in his hand. He stared at it vacantly.

My mother followed Gerald out to the Land Rover and I heard her shout advice after him as the door slammed shut and the convoy of vehicles sped off.

I fell back down onto the pillow, unable to comprehend what had happened. My head felt as big and as thick as a turnip, and my tongue was glued to the top of my mouth. My father looked in at me from the landing and said, 'Get up and see to your mother.'

He fixed me with a stare of such intensity and passion that I thought he was going to throw the piece of metal he had in his hand at me. Instead, he went into his bedroom and I immediately got up and dressed. Downstairs, my mother was sitting by the fire in which a low light was already flickering, and Mrs Heaney from next door was making tea.

'Ah, there you are, Lawrence. Such a thing to have happening and you only home on your holidays. Here, take that wee sup of tay. Yeez are all in shock, God bless us.'

I sat opposite my mother. She had her dressing gown on and her hair was down. I couldn't remember the last time I'd seen her hair like that. It made her face look rounder, younger. 'Where's your father?' she asked in a voice so faint it was hard to believe she had been screaming only moments before.

'Upstairs.'

I felt awful. The hangover made my head thump and I could hardly speak. I held the teacup in my hand and tried to shake myself. The awful incompetence I always felt when I was at home deepened, and I couldn't think straight. It must have been shock, just as Mrs Heaney said.

My father came into the room. He was dressed and he began to put on his boots.

'Where are you going?' asked my mother.

'After Gerald. Down to the Strand Barracks, after Gerald.'

Then he got up and took his coat off the hook by the scullery door. Mrs Heaney stood there with a mug of tea in her hand for him, but he ignored her.

There was a light tap on the front door and Mick Gallagher came into the room. He just stood there, the collar of his leather jacket turned up, his hair swept back as I had seen him the night before. He was wide awake and only his slightly bloodshot eyes showed he might have been hung over.

'I just heard about Gerry,' he said. 'They took three other boys as well. They've probably gone to Castlereagh direct, but we'll find out.' His voice was calm and slow. He was very different from the jovial character I had spoken to at the quiz. 'I'll come back to ye later on. If you could get back to bed, that would be the best thing. I know it's hard to do that now, but it would be the best thing. We'll get someone to fix the door and any other damage there is. No point in even complaining to the Brits about it.'

'I'll fix the door,' my father said. 'I'll do that.' His face was full of pent-up emotion and passion. He looked like he would explode.

'Okay, Mr Mahon,' said Gallagher.

Then he nodded his goodbyes and Mrs Heaney said, 'There now, take that mug of tea now.'

My father took it and stood there in his overcoat and boots as the fury visibly drained out of him. He looked tired and old.

'Go back to bed, Lawrence,' my mother said, and as if in response I gave a yawn, despite my attempts to stifle it.

I got up and my father caught my eye. Now there was almost a sneer in his look, an accusation and a threat. I passed him and made it up the stairs and back to bed too hung over, too confused to wonder why I was being blamed for Gerald getting lifted by the police.

*****

Nobody in the family got to see Gerald for four days. Until the day of his court appearance, the police kept saying that he wasn't asking to see a solicitor. Then my mother and father went to Belfast and had a brief word with him. He was charged with membership of the Provisional IRA as well as attempted murder based on a grenade incident in which a soldier was wounded. For that he could get up to twenty years.

'He looked so pale,' said my mother when she came home.

'Had he been beaten?' I asked.

'He didn't say. He looked all right. Just pale,' she said.

'Don't you know he was beaten? They all are.' My father still boiled inside. The build-up of anger subsided slightly every now and again, but then it would rise to near eruption. His face was red and his neck muscles gorged and tense.

'I suppose he knew what he would be letting himself in for,' I said.

'Oh, he knew all right. And he'll know all about it when he gets twenty years.'

'I don't understand. I mean we're not even a Republican family. How could he...'

'You don't understand!' my father snapped with heavy irony. 'You with your big education and all the world you've seen, you don't understand! Damn right you don't understand. You've been running off out of this town for far too long even to understand what's going on in this house, not to mind anywhere else.'

'Sean!' My mother raised her voice. 'Haven't we enough trouble now, with Gerald in prison, without starting on Lawrence?'

'At least Gerald would've stayed here.' My father sat back into a chair by the fire and put his face in his hands.

I didn't know what to think. He had never spoken to me like that before, and I felt betrayed. Didn't they know what I was going through? Gerald, even if he did do it, and I still couldn't believe he did, had only wounded a soldier. Some people could even see that as a legitimate act of war. I had actually killed a boy, as far as I was concerned. I was senior to Ilpe. I was the engineer. It was my survey we were on. I was to blame, even though he was the driver.

And then I almost told them. I was pent-up like my father and in the living room that evening as they sat opposite each other before the fire, and plates of food Mrs Heaney had cooked going cold on the table, I almost told my father and my mother. About the boy and the mud, and the crunch and Ilpe's white knuckles and the earthslip. But I held back. Something about the vacancy of my mother's stare and the abject look of my father, his face in his hands, made me stop.

Then Mick Gallagher came in and he began to talk to them about Gerald's remand and the likely way things would go for him. I took their dinners back into the kitchen, saying I would reheat them later.

'How are you feeling about all this? Bit of a shock, and you just home.' I hadn't heard Gallagher come into the scullery behind me. After putting my parents' dinner plates in a low oven, I had begun to dry and put away dishes in an absentminded fashion.

'Aye. I suppose. More for me Ma and Da really.'

'They'll find their own strength. And people will rally round them. Families like this one are the backbone of the struggle.'

I stared at him and realised he meant it. It wasn't rhetoric with him. Though we were standing a couple of feet apart in the tiny scullery, though we were about the same age, had grown up on neighbouring streets and done a lot of the same things, I felt a gulf separated us. And what did that mean for the gulf between me and my brother? Between me and my parents?

'I'm not sure I'm part of that struggle.'

'I know. That's the way these things go. Some people resist. Some people don't. Some people, they're not sure. I suppose they wonder about it all. He's still your brother.'

'Where I work, people line up in front of trucks and Land Rovers to stop them going into the forest. Local people. No arms. Resisting, I suppose.'

'I read about that. They must be very brave people. I hope they can keep it up. Only I hope no-one gets killed. I hope they don't have to face their Bloody Sundays.'

It was on the tip of my tongue to tell him then. Here was the sort of person who would understand death. Violent death. The dead boy. Just a boy. Nothing glorious or gallant. Sort of a road traffic accident in a way. I would tell him everything, but then I hesitated.

'Like you say. Some people resist and some people wonder. I saw... I... A boy was killed at one of the barricades. A small boy, and I'm left wondering why. And now my brother is going to jail and all I can do is wonder.'

'That's okay too. It's all part of it.'

Again I saw he meant it. He wasn't just being kind. I wanted to say something about not being so sure about that, but the pressure of the moment took over as someone called his name, and he lifted his hands to me to take his leave and I turned to stare out of the scullery window at the whitewashed wall of the yard, the coal bunker and the drum filled with kindling, a dinner plate cold as death in my hand.

*****

I left on Monday as planned. There seemed no point in staying. My mother was in a daze maintained by Valium. My father froze me out. Mick Gallagher and Mrs Heaney handled everything for them. There wasn't any role for a big brother, especially one like me, an engineer with no knowledge of politics or war.

I made all sorts of promises at the door as I left. I said I would be home at Christmas. I said I would write more regularly. I said I would come home immediately if there was any news of Gerald.

I hugged my mother and felt her bony frame against me. I nodded at my father and he said, 'Good luck.' Then I picked up my bags and carried them to the waiting taxi. I looked back at my parents and at the street where I had been raised. I wanted to fix them in my memory, as if I was convinced I would never see them again.

PART THREE

Forest

CHAPTER EIGHT

My most vivid memory of the journey back to Borneo is of the gruesome food served on the airlines. Congealed lumps of meat and vegetables, which were meant to be appetising and nourishing but were simply unsightly and bland. I pushed them around on the tray until the hostess took them away, and then I slept through the in-flight film. I had no appetite for anything. I was still trying to figure out what exactly I had done to make my father hate me.

And then we landed in Kuala Lumpur and the tropical heat reclaimed me. I was the forest company engineer, back from leave, the professional eager to be back at work. I took a taxi straight to the Searwood office in the city centre. The company occupied three floors of a mid-sized high rise in the commercial sector of the city. The administration and trading needs of camps like mine all over the region were run from there. I had visited it only once before, on my way out to the camp in early 1991. There was no real need for me to visit more often. That was Arkland's job.

I took a lift to the tenth floor and walked to the reception area. I told the Malay woman on the desk who I was, and asked to see Joe Demonti, head of logging operations. This was the tricky bit. There was absolutely no reason why I should be coming to see him. And there was no way I could openly admit that I wanted to find out how much he knew about the death of the boy. I wanted to know if Arkland had been in touch with him. I wanted to know if the police had been in touch. I wanted to know if I still had a job.

'If you'll just wait for a few moments, Mr Demonti will see you.' The receptionist smiled at me and directed me to an arrangement of leather-covered sofas and chairs surrounding a low table made from a slab of timber hewn from one of the big trees. Seraya, I guessed. Varnished and polished with a clear lacquer finish, it carried a spray of glossy timber trade and international business magazines.

I sat down, pushing my bag behind my chair, and picked up a timber trade magazine. I flipped through it in a distracted manner, my mind still somewhere between my home town and Kuala Lumpur. I wondered how Gerald was. I had no idea what things would be like for him. I had nothing to base my imaginings on. I thought of him being beaten and found it fantastical. I thought of him being harassed and shouted at. Scenes from TV crime shows were all I had to go on. It was even harder for me to imagine him involved in a shooting or bombing. My mind couldn't get to grips with that at all.

I looked up from my magazine to the framed photos from the forest that hung on the walls. They showed scenes of logging-company activity. A swathe of road lay across a stretch of forest, and a Mack was positioned on the lip of a hill, three huge logs strapped by steel cables to its powerful back. Another one showed a close-up of the grille of a Mack and three yellow-helmeted loggers leaning against an enormous wheel. A more lyrical one showed a forest stretching away to green-covered hills shrouded in mist. And beside that, the final one showed a tug steaming out to a large ship at anchor in a blue bay. Behind the tug, a raft of the great logs swam like a shoal of marine creatures, while the sunlight spangled on the sea.

I imagine it must have been jet-lag, because I suddenly felt incredibly tired. I began to think it had been a bad idea to come to visit the office, but there was no way out for me now. I felt as if I could sleep for days. Stress, I suppose. A desire to avoid going back to face the camp. And Arkland.

The receptionist was speaking on the phone and when she'd finished she gestured to me that I could go through to the main suite of offices. I crossed the reception area and pushed through a glass door. At the end of a short corridor, I came to Demonti's office and I knocked gently before letting myself in.

Demonti was sitting behind his desk with his back to the

window. An air-conditioning unit stuck out of the wall behind him and made a furious hum. He looked up at me and waved at a chair in front of him.

'Larry Mahon. A wild man from Borneo. Have a seat. What can we do for you?'

I was reminded of how charming and friendly he was. It was known that he considered people like me, who worked in the field, as the real linchpins of the organisation. 'My role is to serve people like you, I guess,' he'd said in his warm Italian New York voice. I knew he'd meant it, which should have made me relax now. But it didn't, and before I could say anything to him, I felt my shins itch to scratching point and I leaned forward to rub them.

'Oh, nothing special. I'm just back from some leave. Passing through, really. Thought I'd call in and say hello.'

If he thought this was an unusually kind gesture on my part, he betrayed no suspicion or annoyance. He clasped his hands behind his head and leaned back in his office chair, bouncing slightly forward and back with an air of someone genuinely glad of a break from the humdrum of work. I didn't envy him the pile of papers and reports that lay across his desk.

'Well, that's real nice of you. You know how I feel about you boys out there in the woods doing the hard work. I wish I was ten years younger and I'd be out there with you. I suppose I had my day. It was time for me to get behind a desk before I did too much damage from behind the wheel of a Mack. Now your boss, Greg Arkland, about time he got himself behind a desk too, eh? Naw. Not Greg. He's too much of a bushwhacker for a job like this.' He gestured disdainfully at the pile of papers on his desk. 'I got something in from him the other day. Should be here.'

He rooted through the pile and I began to sweat, panicking at the thought of what would be in the report.

'Here it is,' Demonti said, flipping through the pages. 'Nothing special seems to have happened while you were away.'

I wanted to see for myself, but Demonti didn't pass the document across to me. He kept absentmindedly reading through it as if he had forgotten I was there.

'Could I see it?' I managed to stumble out. 'Sort of catch up before I finally get back there.'

Demonti passed the report to me, a slightly puzzled look on his face. I suppose he thought I was being particularly keen. 'Did you have a good leave? Everything fine at home?'

'Fine,' I answered him absentmindedly as I furiously pored over Arkland's report. My vision was blurred with excitement. My hands, sopping with sweat, smudged the pages as I raced through them, searching for any hint of the boy being killed. But there was nothing but the usual collection of details of logs felled, cubic metres of timber shipped, and projections, with a map of the next phase, a note about problems with spare parts for the Cats, and a short complaint to the company accountants about money.

'Seems okay. Nothing out of the ordinary, as you say.'

The puzzled look on his face deepened as I put the papers back on his deck. I just wanted to be out of the office, but I managed not to rush, even though I wanted nothing more than to bolt for it.

'Well,' I said, standing up, 'I'll let you get back to your work.'

'Sure, Larry.' Demonti looked genuinely bemused at my sudden desire to leave. He had obvious wanted to settle into a cosy chat about life in the camp. 'You staying tonight? Maybe we could go for a drink. Shit, I just remembered. We're going to dinner with the Beresfords. Maybe a snort after work?'

'I… I'm feeling really bushed, to be honest. Think I'll just go to the hotel and crash out. Try to catch up on some sleep.'

He focused hard on me, inclining his head to one side as he asked, 'Everything all right with you, Larry? You know, if you've got something bugging you, this is the place to leave it. Don't carry it around with you.'

He was the best possible person to talk to about the whole affair. He would really be an ally. He cared for people like me. And he had power. Unlike my father, he would understand. Unlike Arkland, he could be relied upon. But I hesitated to speak to him, still holding to the notion that keeping the whole thing quiet was the best way to deal with it. I judged that if Arkland hadn't mentioned the incident in his report, it should be kept that way. Maybe it would have all blown over when I got back.

'Everything's fine,' I said with a laugh, trying to lighten the seriousness of his enquiry. 'I'm carrying nothing around with me. No secrets, no hidden passions. No great worries. Just a bit jet-lagged. Nothing a good shower and a night between clean sheets won't sort out.'

I'd won him over, because he grinned up at me and said, 'With something warm to cling to between those nice clean sheets.'

I grinned back at him, relieved we had made it back to 'good old boy' chat, as I reached across to take his hand. I noticed him react to the amount of sweat on my palm, but I managed to turn and leave the room before he could question me again.

I took a few moments to settle down in the reception area. I had a sense of almost making a fool of myself. I also had a sense of letting another opportunity to tell my story go by. I wasn't convinced of the wisdom of this, but it still seemed the best course of action. Why face up to something when I didn't have to?

I was picking up my bag when I heard voices from the inner corridor, and two young men came into the reception area. I brightened up when I realised that one of them was Ivor Lewis, an Englishman who had joined the company graduate-induction programme at the same time as me. I knew the other man was American when I heard him say, 'Okay, Ivor baby. Let's get started. You said you were going to show me around this town.'

But Lewis had seen me and he came over, his hand extended in front of him. 'Larry Mahon! I haven't seen you in years. Port Moresby, wasn't it?'

'Hello, Ivor. It has been a long time. Are you posted here now?'

'That's right. Past six months. Sort of holding a few young boys by the hand. Like Graeme here. Graeme Tyson. Larry Mahon.'

The American and I shook hands, nodding at each other.

'What has you at HQ, Larry? I thought you never left the forest. Didn't have any time for the niceties of city life. Jesus, I remember you in Papua. We could hardly get you to come in for a wash.'

Then he continued, turning to the American. 'See this fellow now? This is your genuine article. A Searwood man right to the heart. But not a company man like me, arse broadening from sitting too many hours behind the desk. No, this is the real McCoy, as you Yanks might say. This is a *real* timber-man.'

'You shouldn't pay much attention to what Ivor has to say. He gets carried away with his own myths.'

The American grinned at me as if to say 'I know what you mean', and then turned to Ivor and said, 'Maybe we could invite this legend along for the night. You are supposed to be settling me in. Be a good idea to get some first-hand information from this guy.'

'Splendid idea, Graeme. What about it, Larry? Bit of grub. Sample the nightlife. A few beers. You're welcome to join us. Where are you staying? Rama Gardens? What if we met you in the bar there at about eight?'

'Hang on. Hang on. I'm not… I haven't anything in this bag that will quite match the natty suit you're wearing.'

Ivor was dressed in a light blue tropical suit made locally from delicate linen. The American had a darker blazer with a suitably colourful shirt and tie over cream-coloured slacks. My own shirt and jeans over sneakers, though clean and neatly pressed courtesy of my mother, seemed decidedly downbeat.

Ivor wouldn't have any of it. 'Nonsense. Part of your mystique, your rather streetwise garb. Besides, Graeme has had enough of my desk-wallah blues. You're just the ticket to give him some real-world angles. And Siti will have no trouble getting an extra friend to come along.'

He left us and went to the desk to make arrangements with the receptionist.

Graeme said, 'Where's your camp then?'

'Borneo, sort of straddling the Sabah/Sarawak border. Greg Arkland's in charge. I'm the engineer and general dogsbody.'

'That's what I'm going to be. Hasn't been finalised where I'm going yet. I'll be honest, the delay is getting me down. I can't wait to get among those trees.'

Up close now I realised how young he looked. Early twenties, I guessed, straight out of an American college probably sponsored by Searwood, a couple of stints on camps near Seattle as part of the course.

'This your first posting to the rainforests?'

'Yep. And like I said, I can't wait.'

By this time Ivor had returned to us, gleefully rubbing his hands together with the announcement that we were all set. We'd meet in the bar of my hotel. Then move on to the night market, the *pasar malam*, where Siti, the receptionist, and some friends would meet us.

'We'll have some food, some talk. Maybe go to a club. Live it up a little.'

I had to admit to myself that it all sounded fine. I suppose I was feeling somewhat excited at the prospect of being able to enthral the new boy with stories of wild days in the forest. And I knew Ivor would enjoy basking in the glory of his timber-camp past, giving himself some wild days before his move behind a desk.

We said our goodbyes and I got a taxi to the hotel, feeling pretty good inside. I had gotten over all my doubts about visiting the office. I had managed to confirm that Arkland was playing down the death of the boy. And I had met with a former colleague who would afford me the chance to impress a new man and enjoy the company of some local women. Home, with its family tensions and house raids, was miles upon miles behind me.

CHAPTER NINE

My two companions were already halfway through their drinks when I joined them in the bar of the hotel later that evening. I had overslept, burrowing down into the fresh sheets after spending ages in the steaming shower, washing off the grime of travel and any last sense of home. I had leapt into the bed, thoroughly pleased with myself to be away once more, and almost immediately had fallen into a deep untroubled sleep. Another quick shower, a brisk shave, a fresh shirt covered with a light jacket, my jeans and sneakers would do fine, and I felt on top of the world. Ready for a night on the town. This is more like it, I thought to myself. This is where I really belong. Overseas with the loggers. In the tropics with the sun and the light. Jesus. How I'd crack up if I had to stay in Derry all the time!

Downstairs I caught a glimpse of myself in mirrors in the plant-packed area near the exit from the lifts. My tan gleamed after the shower and shave. My jacket was well filled by my broad shoulders. I looked slim and strong, with enough body in my hair to make it lift across my forehead gracefully.

Now Ivor waved at me and I crossed the bar to where they were sitting in a nest of seats in front of a huge palm plant. There were hidden lights that served to provide intimate spaces in the open bar. In the distance, I got a view of a swimming pool, completely empty of people now, the water shimmering merrily on the glass walls and high ceiling.

'Gin okay for you?' Ivor called and then, before I could answer, raised three fingers to the man behind the bar.

I pulled up a chair beside them and settled into it. Almost immediately, a young Malay woman came with our drinks. There was a ritualistic silence as she put down three little mats bearing the hotel's logo, one in front of each of us. Then, dipping and moving with professional grace, she placed our drinks before us. Three tall glasses, clear liquid bubbling inside them, a sliver of lemon neatly balanced on the edge of each glass, a slim swirl-stick rising out of the clump of ice-cubes that bobbled in the drink.

'I got you the same as us, Larry. Should be all right. Cheers.'

I took my first sip, wondering if Ivor and Graeme had been at it for long. They both wore the same clothes they had had on earlier, and I guessed they'd gone straight from the office to one of Ivor's haunts before coming here to join me.

'See? I told you, Larry. I knew you'd find something to put on. You look positively charming. Almost civilised. But not quite. Excellent.'

I thanked him and took another sip from my drink.

'So how is it out in the camp these days?' Ivor winked at me as he asked. I guessed he wanted me to reply in as colourful a fashion as I could. Give the young American something to get his teeth into. My own feeling was that, young as he was, Graeme was no fool, but I decided to give Ivor something to enjoy.

'Same as it's always been, Ivor. You'll know that. You've served your time. You may be behind a desk now but you've had enough leeches crawl up your arse to know a thing or two.'

Ivor grinned across at me so I knew I was on the right track. Then Graeme asked, 'Is it true that no matter what you do, boots or socks, creams or whatever, you just can't keep them away from you?'

'Pretty much. I've tried all sorts of stunts. Some of the local remedies work a bit, but no matter where I've been, the locals just seem to put up with them and get on with things. I've found that's the best way myself. Try to ignore them.'

I found myself enjoying the sound of my own voice. Showing off a little in front of this new recruit. Ivor was basking in the reflected glory of having set up the meeting. He'd promised 'the real thing' and I had turned up out of the blue and right on cue. I was glad to see him pleased and I was glad of the attention and the distraction. I ordered a round of drinks and the waitress brought them, serving us with the same precise and ritualised movements, her head bowed so as to avoid eye contact, lifting and bending between us as we reclined in our seats, masters of our time and place. We were young men overseas, working for a multinational company. White, rich and powerful.

I watched her move away, running my eyes over her elegant back to her legs encased in sheer black tights. I felt the alcohol loosen me up and felt a stirring in my groin that made me think of Bronagh. I smiled to myself and privately raised my glass to her and the time at Claire's wedding, wishing her well in a distant kind of way. That's how it's always been with me. Women as far-away objects, more of admiration than desire. More to be avoided than to know.

I wondered if Graeme had read my mind when he asked, 'I suppose there are no women at the camps?'

Ivor guffawed and I smiled serenely. 'No. No women. Only the ones in your head.'

We continued to banter like that for another round. I told tales of snakes in the bed. Scorpions in boots. Drinking binges. Men killed in tree-felling. Vehicles crashing. Roads subsiding. Rain falling in Old Testament deluges. Graeme listened avidly. Ivor threw in his own short amplifications and comments, keeping himself associated with my yarns, maintaining his position as my friend who, even though he had gone the route of the administrator, still had enough forest-cred behind him to be worthy of note. Finally he announced that we should make a move. 'Can't keep the girls waiting. Said we'd be there about now. Bit of supper. Never know what that might lead to, eh, Larry?'

We met the women at the *pasar malam*. There was Siti, the receptionist, and her two friends, Sadah and Amra. They were all Malay women, working with international companies, Sadah with IBM and Amra with another timber company whose name I missed. Ivor seemed to get on particularly well with Siti, and they adopted the role of leaders, with Graeme and me falling in with Sadah and Amra. We walked down the colourfully lit streets of the night market, stopping every now and then to browse at the stalls. There were batiks and other clothes. Sadah held a sarong with a design of marvellously plumed birds against her, and we all laughed in admiration. Then we came to the area of the market given over to eating stalls. The smells were wonderful. Each stall looked as marvellous as the next one. Small groups of local people sat enjoying the exquisite food. Graeme, Ivor and I were the only white people I could see, and that added to my feeling of being special. One of the anointed. One of the leaders working on the frontier.

The women enjoyed discussing the merits of various stalls until finally settling on one. We took our seats and advice flowed around the table. Graeme was the focus of most of this. I sensed that he was relishing the role of new boy just as much as I was relishing being the old hand. Ivor acted as ringmaster.

'Come on, Siti. Ready to drop with hunger here. Let's just get some satay. You've never had that before, have you, Graeme? Essential part of the experience, isn't it, Larry?'

I nodded in agreement. Satay would be fine with me. We were seated at a table near the barbecue on which the stallholder was grilling the small strips of meat skewered on thin sticks. The smell of grilling meat made my stomach rumble and I looked about me, transfixed by the awe I felt at being in such a place. Me, with my Da a carpenter on building sites. My mother tied to the house. And my brother in prison. Here I was in a market stall in Kuala Lumpur, under a lightly flapping awning, gaily coloured bulbs strung around us to light our cosmopolitan party, grinning at myself in self-amazement.

Siti gave our orders and suddenly our table became laden with dishes of food. There were plates for each of us. Two mounds of steaming rice were placed in the centre of the table. Side dishes of fish and vegetables and an assortment of beef and chicken satay arrived. There were dishes of the heated peanut sauce that accompanied the satay, and Amra made great efforts to explain to Graeme the proper way of eating the dish. The women expressed delight at seeing me wash my fingers and eat in the local manner. Again I was being the old hand, and great hilarity was experienced at Graeme's faltering efforts to use his fingers.

Ivor beamed in delight. The party was turning out to be a rip-roaring success. I saw him share intimate pleasantries with Siti. Every time she whispered something to him he burst out laughing. I could see him in five years' time settled down here. A new house in one of the finer suburbs. A permanent fixture at the office. Happily growing fat and comfortable. Memories of rain-sodden home fading. Could that be me?

A neat pile of satay sticks lay beside me, and I began to play with them. Rolling them together. Making a mesh by overlaying them. Sectioning them off in terms of length and then in terms of quality. I would soon be going back to work. This was only a respite. I would be back in the forest and this cosmopolitan interlude would fade just as quickly as the images of my time at home. I struggled to bring up clear pictures of the wedding. The nights out with Gerald. The house raid.

Graeme was laughing. Sadah and Amra, on either side of him, were trying to teach him some Malay. His foolish mispronunciations caused great laughter. There was an innocence about him that reminded me of myself when I had first gone overseas. It had all been a novelty to me then. All an adventure. I still felt a bit like that, but I seemed to be more tired. As if I had lost my innocence. It was the boy, I told myself. Killing the boy had done that to me.

Under the awning that separated us from the next stall I could see a pair of brown legs. A boy's. The legs moved between the tables, obviously serving the diners. Then they moved towards the front of the stall where another satay barbecue was set up. I saw a boy of about ten. From the back I could see his clean T-shirt and grey school shorts. An older brother was turning sticks of satay on the barbecue, and the younger boy filled a dish once more, then ladled some sauce into a little bowl before making his way back among the tables when once again I had to follow the passage of his legs. Young and strong. It was Gerald. And I was making the satay. We were a team, brothers, and I was looking after him. Keeping him right. Guiding him. Just as the satay maker was. Calling again in a firm but gentle voice. Giving directions. Advising on presentation and quantity. Working together.

On his next visit back to the barbecue, the boy turned round to pick up a squat bottle of soy sauce. He faced into our area and, catching my eye, he smiled, showing rows of even white teeth and a lock of black hair lolling over his forehead. I tried to smile back at him but I felt my stomach heave. The boy turned away and I knew that if I didn't get up immediately I would vomit over everybody at the table.

'Excuse me. Got to...'

I pushed back my chair and dashed from the stall. My head was starting to spin and gulping retches convulsed my insides. I looked back at the table to see the others stare after me in amazement. Ivor stood up and seemed about to follow, but I never found out if he did because I ran along the line of stalls, pushing past people who stood in wonder. Vomit filled my mouth and I knew that I would not be able to hold back the retching for much longer, so in desperation I ran behind the stalls and, bending over, I released the pent-up food and bile and alcohol. My forehead was covered in sweat. My stomach felt as if I had been kicked. I spat the last of the rotten bile from my mouth and rubbed the back of my hand across my mouth.

Suddenly the awning beside me was lifted and the outraged face of a Chinese stallholder screamed at me. Behind him I could see tables of diners, appalled at what they had seen and heard. The man gesticulated and pointed, his wispy white beard bobbing on his chin as he screamed at me. I mumbled apologies and staggered away from him, turning at the corner of the food stalls and running as fast as I could back through the market until I came to the main road and managed to feel more secure among the evening traffic.

I walked and walked then, not even noticing the streets. My head was bowed. My feet dragged me along. I brushed pieces of satay from my jacket and my shirt. I was disgusted with myself.

It wasn't the gin. I told myself I wasn't even drunk. Jesus, what was wrong with me? Would I be running away forever? Was this all I could do now?

I came to the centre of the city and stood on the banks of the river at the spot from which the city takes its name. There are two rivers running together and a small mosque sitting on a promontory at the confluence. Kuala Lumpur. The muddy confluence. That's where I was.

CHAPTER TEN

The next day I caught the first available flight to Borneo. As soon as I landed, I took a taxi to the railway station, where I put a call through to the camp and caught the afternoon train to Beaufort. I hadn't stopped running since I had left the food stall. I didn't contact the office. Shame and panic kept me moving.

Ilpe met me in the Land Rover as planned, a perk for the *orang puteh*, the white man. Gaing, the head logger, was with him and the back of the Land Rover was full of supplies. Rice, cooking oil, chains for the saws, batteries for torches. Driving onto the metal bridge over the Sungei Padas, I managed to smile to myself as I remembered the story Gaing had told me about the Second World War.

'Japanese *puchong,* you know, cocks. My father and his people string them across a log further up river and sail them down here. Japanese very unhappy.'

We bumped off the bridge onto the rough dirt road that took us out of the town, past the rubber plantations and away into the hills and the rainforest. I saw the tree-topped peaks ahead of me, and I realised seeing them made me feel good. But I knew I would have to ask Ilpe about the boy, though I was trying to not even think about it. He must have read my mind because he said, 'The police have come to the camp. About the boy. They asked me questions. And Mr Arkland. Then they left. Mr Arkland said they were looking for you.'

'What did the police say to you?'

'Nothing much. Just said they would be back.'

Then a lizard ran out of the bush on the right-hand side of the road, and Ilpe accelerated forward, careering over the bumpy surface in an effort to run it over. Gaing shouted encouragement, waving furiously, but the lizard made it across, slithering finally into the bush as we scraped the branches, scattering water and mud from the rutted surface of the road.

Gaing and Ilpe laughed and shouted about how close a thing it had been. Lizard meat was highly prized at the camp. I couldn't join in the excitement. Normally I would have enjoyed the chase. But now I felt I was the lizard. If I ever got away, I was certain I would be chased again.

*****

Two days later I was at my desk when I heard Arkland's uneven tread on the boards. He came into my office, followed by a policeman.

'This is Sergeant Merkat,' said Arkland. 'He wants to talk to you.'

It was the first time I had seen Arkland since my return. He had been away in the capital when I had got back. Now I wanted to talk to him before being confronted by the policeman. But he ushered Sergeant Merkat in and slammed the door closed as he left.

The policeman came forward and sat in the chair opposite me.

'You will have to come with us, Mr Mahon. We have to ask you some questions at the station. Your driver also.'

I almost laughed at this effrontery, but somehow the stare in Sergeant Merkat's eyes convinced me that this would not have been a good idea.

'Some questions? What… What… What do you mean?' I couldn't help it. I was stammering.

'Mr Mahon. A boy has been killed. We have received a report. You and your driver were in the Land Rover at the time. You will come to the police station to answer questions. Simple, eh?' He leaned towards me and continued, 'We can force you to come, Mr Mahon, but you know that would be a bad idea for both of us. Just some questions.'

I wanted desperately to speak to Arkland, so I got up and walked out of the office. There was a police Land Rover parked opposite me. I could see Ilpe seated in the back between two policemen. I turned towards Arkland's office and a group of policemen came along the boardwalk to me. Behind me I heard Sergeant Merkat's voice call something, and the policemen grabbed me and bundled me across to their Land Rover.

I couldn't believe what was happening. I started to shout and to thrash about. I called out to Arkland, but no-one came. I was shoved into the back of the Land Rover beside Ilpe, and calmed down, overcome by disbelief and fear. Then we drove away at high speed. Ilpe looked at me. 'It will be all right. They just want to ask us some questions.'

*****

When I recall the next forty-eight hours, I see them as a scene from the film *The Count of Monte Cristo*. The isolation, the banishment, the lonely cell. I found myself imagining I would never be free. And I couldn't get it out of my mind that my parents now had both sons in police custody. I knew I shouldn't have been there. I did feel in some way responsible for the death of the boy. But I wasn't a murderer.

They took us to the little town on the coast, near the timber camp. The police station was in a cluster of government buildings, all on stilts, along the shore. I was put in a cell with a low bed and a high window for light and air. Ilpe was in the next cell to me, on the other side of a thick wall. I couldn't believe this was happening to me. I kept waiting for Arkland to come and bail me out. Whenever a policeman passed my cell, I shouted at him to open the door, to let me get in touch with a solicitor, to let me contact Arkland at the camp. But I was ignored. I was told to slop out and I was fed.

I spent the time watching a gecko on the wall of my cell. There was nothing particularly unusual about this little lizard. I was used to hundreds of them all over the place. I suppose it was the time I had. So I would lie on my bunk and observe it scurrying about, chasing the flies that were drawn into the cell when the light was on. I tried to map out its paths and decided that, while they were generally random, a primitive pattern could be seen. Certain routes dominated. Certain areas seemed to be out of bounds, as if the gecko knew its limits. It scurried towards the window but never far enough so that it could see out. Then it spun round and raced back to the gap in the plaster that led into the roof space it occupied during most of the day. I tried to predict where it would go. I tried to guess what it would do, and I found myself racing with it across the wall, scurrying ahead of it, trying to stay within my limits, hoping everything would be sorted out without having to go too far out of the ordinary. I watched its rippled and mottled back, its suction-cupped feet, its darting eyes and swishing tail, and I saw myself as that lizard. I was trying to stay within my limits. I was trying to keep things under control but I was also wandering about randomly, as if searching for something.

A door would slam somewhere and the gecko would stall for an instant, shiver and cling even more tightly to the wall, then cast its tail – its only defensive device – before scurrying furiously to its hideaway. Tail-less.

I found myself thinking back on my journeys around the world and pictured how life would have been different if I had stayed at home. I certainly wouldn't have been in this mess, but maybe I would have ended up like Gerald. Involved.

Come you home from school and get that homework done. That way you'll not be knackered in the morning for swimming. Let them other boys go down to the rioting. That's not for you, son. It's for the best if you go away after. There's nothing for you here only bother.

My father's words ran through my brain like an electric current. Something about the mournful tone of them. Something of an apology in them, as if he was accepting adult responsibility for the Troubles. As if he was saying that he wanted things to be different, but didn't know how to make that happen.

There's no work in it anyway. Not unless you want to be become a cop.

He said that later, with a bit of a mocking laugh in his voice. We were in the back yard. I was home from Queen's, just after my finals in 1984, certain of getting a good degree and with a number of job options, including the Searwood one, ahead of me.

He was chopping kindling for the fire. A regular weekly chore. He brought short lengths and ends of wood home every few days and threw them into a box in the yard. Then over the weekend he would spend an hour chopping the lengths into small pieces, which he stored in a drum next to the coal bunker. He used a neat hatchet, with a fine hazelwood handle, that had belonged to his father. The whorls on the wood seemed to match the whorls on his thumb wrapped round the handle. He worked methodically with an easy stroke.

Thinking back on the scene from my prison cell, with the gecko scurrying happily and the soft lulling sound of waves breaking on the beach outside, I saw it as a scene of great peace and quiet, even though the hatchet made a splintering thud every time he drew it down. Even though the sounds of rioting could be heard two streets away. The calling and the sirens. The explosive splat of petrol bombs landing. The grim thump of plastic rounds being fired. 'Your mother'll miss you wild,' he said, bringing the hatchet down and splitting a piece of white wood from an end of skirting board so that the bare flesh showed white and jagged. I tried to catch his eyes to get some hint that maybe he would miss me too, but he concentrated on his wood-chopping, bringing down the hatchet and tossing the new kindling into the drum beside the coal bunker. My mind filled up with questions but I couldn't ask any of them. They crowded my mouth and tasted like the wood chippings dusted about my father's feet.

So I became the gecko scurrying around the world looking for something, yet never really sure what it was, never really daring to make a real break for it, a real dash for glory. These thoughts ranged about me as I lay on my bunk and forced the questions back into my mind.

Will you miss me, Father? Am I doing the right thing?

'Why won't you ask me to stay?' I spoke out loud and the gecko spun and dashed away at the sound of my voice. When he reappeared, he was cautious and alert, tentative and wary. He remained close to the corner where his lair was. I began to fear that he would go hungry because I had spoken out loud, and added that thought to the mountain of regrets I had piling up inside me. When I finally turned to the wall and scrunched the sheet around me to try to sleep, great gulping sobs shook me.

*****

I continued to be ignored until Sergeant Merkat finally came back and took my statement. I told him everything I knew. Just as it happened. The rain, the human barricade, the Land Rover slewing in the mud, the boy running, the mother reaching, the awful scrunching sound, the engine revving, me shouting 'Stop', Ilpe driving.

Sergeant Merkat took it all down in a flowing longhand. 'And you stopped to render assistance?' he asked.

'We drove… Ilpe drove on. Then he finally stopped some distance further up the road.'

'And then you turned back to the boy?'

'No. We stopped and I got out.'

'Why?'

I couldn't explain to him. How could I tell him I got out because my father's voice was ringing in my head?

'To compose myself.'

Sergeant Merkat's pen hovered over the page, before he wrote my answer and said, 'Go on please.'

I continued to the point of returning to the camp and Sergeant Merkat put down his pen and said that would be all.

I demanded to see a lawyer.

'But why a lawyer, Mr Mahon?' he said. 'You are a free man. Just as I said. Some questions. That is all.'

By the time we were driven back up to the camp later that day, a new emotion had been added to my increasing stock. It was puzzlement. I couldn't wait to see what part Arkland had played in this. I wondered why Arkland had abandoned me. Gaing was there to meet us. He told me Arkland was away for a few days. There was a note on my desk from him. It gave full details of a road problem, but made no mention of my being in police custody. He would be in the capital for a few days and expected I would cope. I wasn't sure if he was being sarcastic with that last remark.

I threw myself into my work immediately. I spent almost four hours after the evening meal in my office poring over maps, catching up on paperwork, preparing work schedules, doing calculations for a new stretch of road we were about to open. I drove myself, and in doing that I drove out everything else – the boy, my brother in prison, my confusion with Arkland and, most of all, the hurt I felt because of what I'd seen in my father's eyes the night Gerald was taken away.

And the next day I rushed from my bed for an early breakfast with the loggers. I wanted to cheat sleep, to keep dreams away by working hard and sleeping little. Then, as dawn was just about to light up the camp and the trucks of loggers pulled out, I climbed into the Land Rover and drove out of the camp. It started to rain again and I had to put on the wipers. They swished at the early monsoon torrents and I strained to see out in front of me. The tail lights of the trucks winked ahead of me until we came to the Kilometre Five fork and I followed the right branch that went down into the valley below us where dawn light hadn't yet reached, and it became harder and harder to control what came and went in my mind. This was so new to me. I had never known anything like this before. I had always been in charge, in control of my mind and my thoughts. And now I was in a crazy half-dream with the dead boy and my brother vying for my attention. I drove on through the mud down into the valley's darkness, begging them to leave me alone. And they went, only to be replaced by the accusing hurtful stare of my father as he stood on the landing with the bent metal in his hand.

I came to the valley floor and the road levelled off. The rain seemed to have stopped and I turned off the wipers. A fine mist-like drizzle kept pattering the windscreen, but I knew that was just the forest raining down to the ground. I came to the end of the road and checked the maps on the seat beside me. Then I drew on my raincoat and stepped out. Mud squelched up the sides of my boots but I didn't care. I had to get out of the Land Rover. Work now was the only thing that could save me from the thoughts inside my head.

The forest round about me was still and dark. Only the dripping of the rain from the leaves high above could be heard. Then, with a crash and a thump, a tree fell far off. A natural fall, marking the end of time for a forest tree and the beginning of its return through detritus and humus to enrich the forest floor from where it had grown hundreds of years before. There would be many more frequent tree falls when I got this road marked out and the loggers came with their squealing chainsaws.

I took a sack of marker sticks from the back of the Land Rover and rechecked the survey sheets I had set on the driver's seat. Satisfied, I walked away from the Land Rover off the road and into the forest where underfoot conditions were a lot better. I placed my first marker, confirmed my bearings and trudged fifty metres to my left to set the second. This would be a good area to log. There were plenty of meranti and seraya, good for logs and just what our customers in Japan wanted. If we could get this sector worked before the full onset of the monsoon season, we would keep ahead of production targets. These were the thoughts, the professional concerns, that occupied me as I moved through the forest, pushing aside the dangling lianas, flicking leeches off my hands, chopping streamers with my parang and placing my markers for the loggers' cutting lines.

It was almost a sixth sense that made me look behind me after I had placed the final marker. I heard no noise but the dripping of the forest. All I could smell were the forest smells. And yet I turned around, convinced there was someone behind me. There was a man standing fifty metres away. He was standing on a fallen log. He wore a loincloth and the heavy earrings on the long earlobes of the Penan people. He had a blowpipe in one hand, and tucked under his other arm he carried my other markers.

My first thought was that I only had my parang. I put my hand to the hilt and squeezed it. How many of them were they? Where were they? How could I get back to the Land Rover? And I knew at once how pointless that thought was. I could be killed or stunned by a poisoned dart fired from where the Penan man stood.

There was a slight rustling beside me, and as I spun round, two other men appeared quite close to me. One of them was the old man I had seen in the camp talking with Arkland. He spoke to me in Malay, but I couldn't make out what he was saying. It was obvious he was ordering me away, back to the camp. I didn't speak enough Malay to answer him, and when he pointed towards the Land Rover, I began to walk, holding my final marker in my hand. I tried to avoid the man holding the other markers, but he crossed over to stand in front of me. Then he said something in his own language and dropped the markers at my feet.

There was the flash and whirr of a self-winding camera as I bent down to pick up the markers. When I stood up, bundling my thin red and white rods under my arm, I was photographed again.

The photographer was a young woman, and as I stared at her, she kept taking my photograph. Then she walked across to where the three Penan men were standing and shouted in English.

'Go back to your camp. These people do not want you here. You are destroying their home and killing their children.'

It was a totally different type of barricade, a totally different action by the Penan. I wouldn't be able to come back here without a gun. I returned to the Land Rover and drove to the camp. I decided to wait until Arkland returned before coming back to open up this new sector. He was the boss, after all.

CHAPTER ELEVEN

It was another three days before Arkland returned. In the meantime, I kept the team deployed in the upland sector, though we were moving too far away from our base. The shift to the valley-floor sector was vital to maximise the use of the camp. I still hadn't figured out how we were going to respond to the new Penan tactics.

I was sleeping in my room when Arkland came in. Humidity was high and so was the midday heat. I had eaten a stew of bush-pig meat for lunch, and was in a deep stupefied sleep full of dreams of naked women performing impossible contortions while straddling me.

'Put an ice-pack on that mad Irish cock of yours, Mahon. Didn't the priests tell you it was sinful to even think about it?'

Arkland clumped across the room and sat on a chair beside the bed.

'I've just got in and I find my right-hand man is beating the meat while the timber trade in Asia goes through the roof. Here, catch up on the news on the home front. I reckon I'll lie down for a stretch too.' He tossed me a letter, got up and left the room.

I hadn't properly come to and never even said a word. I half-raised myself off the bed, but as I heard his footfalls recede down the boardwalk, I slumped back down. Then I looked at the letter lying across my sweaty chest. It had been posted in Derry the day after I left. The small round letters sloping away from the pen told me so much about my mother. The capital Ps looked so like her, pert bun on top included.

It was the most abject letter I had ever received from my mother, because in it she apologised for Gerald getting lifted and the way that had spoiled my holiday. How I pitied my mother then. She had spent most of her life, all her adult life, deferring to three men. Me, my brother and my father. She was always trying to make things right for us. She said my father was out of his state of shock. She said she was coping much better. Mrs Heaney had been great. So had Mick Gallagher. Gerald was charged with attempted murder and membership of the IRA. She gave no further details of the charges. I remembered that it was for a shooting or a grenade attack, but no matter how much I tried to understand it as I lay there, the fan vainly stirring the muggy air, I still couldn't get to grips with my brother. My younger brother whom I had taught to swim and who had hero-worshipped me when I competed in inter-town galas. I remembered him up in the spectator gallery, waving down at me as the prizes were presented. He could get life, my mother wrote, and the fear and pain I had felt at my own imprisonment came back to me. He was on remand, she wrote, and added that Mick Gallagher had said he could be like that for months. It's another form of internment without trial, he'd said.

I put the letter onto the floor beside the bed, wishing at that moment that I had never received it. It required me to do something. At least to write a consoling reply. I didn't need anything to revitalise the demons in my head just as I was beginning to get on top of them. And I had my own problems to contend with. The boy's death was still not closed off. And the Penan in the valley sector. Judging by his tone of voice, Arkland would be more interested in the progress with work than in my family problems. But I was wrong, because when I went to see him in his office later that afternoon, the first thing he asked about was my family.

'You got parents? Still alive?' He started to shake his head as I nodded. 'Mine are both dead. I've got no kin really. Funny that? Maybe that's why I've stayed out here. No good reason to go home.'

I lied to him that everything was fine at home and he said, 'Good, good, glad to hear it.' He was standing in front of his beloved maps, rearranging the pins in yet another display that no-one but himself could understand.

'Any progress down the valley?' He shifted two more pins as he spoke.

I told him about my markers being taken and the Penan headman ordering me away. I told Arkland I was waiting to have a word with him before deciding what I might do next.

'So,' he said, gazing at the new sector on his maps. 'They're going to stop us, eh? They're going to up the stakes a bit, are they? And have you figured out how we're going to handle this?'

'I thought I'd talk it over with you first before taking any action.'

'A wise move, Mahon. A bang-on-the-bulls-eye move. Let's get a drink. I got some hooch while I was up in the capital, so it wasn't a totally wasted trip.'

He opened a drawer on his desk and lifted out a bottle of Jack Daniels. He pulled off the plastic covering and poured two large measures into tin mugs he took from the same drawer. 'How long you been here now?' he said.

'Same as you almost. I came three weeks after the concession opened. Over a year ago.'

'Not long,' he mused. 'Still, it's not your first time in the forests. You've seen more places than me in your short career. Bottoms up.'

We clinked cups and I sipped the bourbon.

'So I guess you know all about epiphytes then, eh? No? No. Why should you? You're a numbers man, an engineer, not a botanist. Well, let me tell you about them. Epiphytes are plants that grow not from the ground, but from other plants. And around us here they grow on the trunks of the trees. They don't hurt the trees they grow on. They're not parasites. In fact, you could say they really do something for the tree. Like orchids. You know them, eh? They're epiphytes, getting their food and water from the big trees. Living off the fat of the forest. That's us too, you know. Me and you. We're epiphytes. Living off the fat of the forest, really adding to the value of the place. Another belt?'

He clinked the bottle off our cups, said 'Bottoms up' again and lurched across to the chair behind his desk. He threw himself into it, backside first. It was the only way I'd ever seen him getting seated. 'If I don't do it this way,' he told me, 'this goddam leg gets in the way and I either end up sitting on it or on my ass on the floor.' He hadn't spilled a drop of the bourbon. 'Yes, Larry Mahon. Epiphytes. That's what we are. Just like the orchids.'

'There was a photographer with them. She took my photo a couple of times.'

'In the forest?'

'Yes.'

'Is she living with them?'

'I don't know. She must be. She told me they wanted me out of the forest.'

'A greennik, would you say? An enviro-freak, eh?'

'Maybe. She's not Penan. Too tall. Definitely an outsider. Like Chinese.'

'Did you get her name?'

'No. We weren't introduced.'

Arkland smiled. He liked the irony, the humour. 'That's right. Even in the most difficult of circumstances it's best to keep up the social niceties. I've always liked that about you, Larry. You're polite. And you know your place.'

I knew I would be wasting my time talking to him any more, so I got up to leave. 'Let's talk about it tomorrow. You must be exhausted after your trip.'

'Okay, Larry,' he said breezily. 'Let's talk about it tomorrow.' I had my hand on the door when he called out, 'And, Larry, if you see that photographer girl again, you tell me, you hear?'

'You're interested in her?'

'She's a woman, isn't she? And you know what it's like out here.'

I knew exactly what it was like. But I wasn't thinking about the photographer in that way, and I didn't believe that Arkland was either. But I couldn't figure out exactly why he seemed so interested in her.

When I got back to my room I took up my mother's letter and

read it once more. Then I sat at my desk and read it again. I tried to conjure up a picture of her as she wrote it, trying to fix everything that surrounded her. I knew exactly where Gerald was. My own period in custody allowed me to guess what it was like for him. I imagined he would probably be roughed up and cajoled and offered deals. 'Sign for this and we'll forget the rest. Give us three names, just three, and we'll quash the evidence on you. Trust us.'

But I couldn't see my father. Or rather, I couldn't seem to pin him down. I couldn't be sure where he was. I wasn't really in touch with him.

*****

I was surprised when Arkland suggested the next day that we would leave the valley sector alone for a while. 'Let's cool it down there for a while. We've got enough to cut up here. Besides, when the monsoon really gets going we won't be able to move down in the valley. We may be talking about shelving that area until the dry season again.'

I had expected him to say we'd go in there all guns blazing, and if the Penan didn't like it, tough shit. 'We'll have to talk some more about this, Greg,' I said. 'We haven't enough trees standing to meet production deadlines without going down to the valley. At least not with our camp based here. We could of course move camp, but I don't know, this time of year wouldn't be good for that and...'

'How long you say you been here, Mahon?' Arkland cut in. 'How long?'

'Eleven, twelve months.'

'One lousy year. I've been in this bloody country four years and elsewhere in these islands, I don't know, maybe fifteen. Let me give it to you straight, Larry boy. I know this place. This is Borneo. Right? Borneo. Not some pretty part of Australia or Amazonia. Those people out there are head-hunters and your head is near the top of their list. If I say we cool it a little, then that's just what we do.'

He was glaring across his desk at me, veins on his cheeks etched like rivulets of blood. I wanted to tell him I didn't trust him any more, not since the moment he turned me over to the police. Why didn't he come for me then? From now on, if he wanted to make decisions about the camp, he would be on his own.

'Okay, Greg. As you say. Let's cool it.'

I left his office and walked straight out into the camp square. The sun was fully up now and the square was bright, though still cool. I blew out the air squeezed up in my lungs and decided I needed some coffee.

Gaing was coming out of the vehicle stockade as I passed on my way to the cookhouse. 'You not going out today?' he asked.

'No.' I didn't know what I was going to do that day. I had been working up to opening that new sector in the valley and would have to think of something else now.

'Good,' said Gaing. 'You can help me with the Cat sometime today maybe?'

'Sure, no problem. Let's get a cup of coffee first.'

I'm a civil engineer by training but in the years on timber camps I've learned enough to be useful when one of the large vehicles breaks down. Gaing, the mechanic, often asked for help, and I liked working with him. We went into the cookhouse. It was dark and smoky. Rice was cooking and Dapo was cleaning the large tables after breakfast. He looked up when he saw us and I said, 'Two coffees.' Dapo muttered something under his breath in Tagalog, and Gaing and I shared a smile.

When the coffee came Gaing said, 'We go down into the valley soon? Before the big rains?'

'No. Maybe not for a while yet.'

'But there is no more timber up high. It is too far from camp now. It is time to go down into the valley.'

Gaing had the sallow, flat face of the local Murut people. Farmers in the hills, they had come readily enough to the timber camps, usually as unskilled chainsaw men. Gaing had learned the rudiments of mechanics from a Filipino in another camp, and could read and write a little. He was unofficial leader of the men, local and Filipino. That he should be of the same opinion as myself only made Arkland's decision seem worse.

'There will be no work for the men,' he continued, 'if we do not go down into the valley.'

'They can go back to the *kampung*,' I said.

'Not without money for rice and meat,' Gaing said.

Then we heard the helicopter. Dapo came out of the kitchen and said something in Tagalog. Gaing shrugged and the three of us went outside in time to see the helicopter land in the square in front of us. Sunlight flashed off the rotors as they slowed down. The passenger door opened and a man in a tropical suit, carrying a briefcase, got out and ran, crouching, to the boardwalk in front of Arkland's office. The pilot then got out, stretched himself and walked over to us.

'*Selemat pagi. Ada kopi, yah?*' he greeted us.

He wore an Air Force uniform and dark glasses. His forehead was slightly creased by the line of his flight helmet.

'Ask him where he's from,' I said to Gaing, and Gaing spoke to the pilot.

'He's from Kuala Lumpur. The Ministry of Forestry. He came over last night with Encik Said bin Mohammed.'

'Encik Said. Is that the fellow gone into Arkland's office?'

'Yes. He is assistant to the Minister.'

'Thanks, Gaing. Tell Dapo to get him some coffee.'

Dapo muttered something under his breath and beckoned the pilot into the cookhouse. I followed Gaing to the vehicle stockade to begin work repairing the track on the Cat. That suited me. I was near at hand if Arkland called me. I didn't really expect him to. Maybe I just wanted to keep an eye on him.

'What do you make of all this then?'

It took me a while to phrase the question that had been running through my mind ever since the helicopter had landed. By now Gaing was already down in the rough pit we used to inspect the underside of our vehicles. His arm reached out and I passed him a socket wrench.

'This pipe is very worn down. Maybe we should replace it

before it blows and the brakes go completely.' His voice was muffled and distant, but I had a sense that he had heard my question all right. His arm appeared again, laying two wrenches and a length of hydraulic fluid pipe, gnarled and shrivelled, beside them. Then he appeared from underneath the vehicle. He stood at the end of the pit, blinking to set his eyes against the glare of the sun, wiping his hands on an oily cloth he pulled from the waistband of his jeans. His upper body was bare, showing his lithe and muscular brown frame streaked with engine fluids and dirt. I might be the engineer, but he was the better mechanic.

'We need to pull them all in,' he said. 'All the vehicles. Give them a good check. Before we have a big accident.'

He was right, of course, but only in the best of worlds. In the narrow world of pushing for greater and greater output, there was no way I could convince Arkland to stand down any vehicle for non-essential repairs. Gaing knew that too, I suppose, because he continued, 'Let's just try to take things easy. Maybe I can work on this Cat later, and if we do hold off the valley sector for a few days, maybe we can get the Macks in.'

'Maybe. Let me see what Arkland says.'

'Arkland doesn't want anything to stop. Not man. Not machine.'

'You don't like him, do you?'

'I just look after the trucks. And I look after the men, I suppose. That's the way the company likes it. Arkland doesn't want me to think too much.'

But I do, I thought to myself. I want to know what you think of this helicopter visit by the man from the Ministry.

Gaing was ahead of me. 'This man, coming from KL in a helicopter. It must mean trouble for Arkland. And if it's trouble for him, then it's big trouble for me and the men.'

That was how I read it too. Arkland wasn't going to let himself get boxed in. I had a funny feeling that Gaing and I should really be friends but something was stopping us. There seemed to be such a degree of common understanding and interest that we ought to be friends, but it was as if Arkland was getting in the way.

'You don't like me either, do you really?'

Gaing raised his eyes from the pipe he had been peering at and leaned against the step of the cab beside him. There was a wide grin on his face.

'The time in prison has made you weak perhaps, Larry Mahon? You don't trust anybody any more. Did I not take you to my *kampung* and let you meet my family? You stayed in my longhouse and ate with my parents. Remember?'

It wasn't quite the answer I hoped for. Maybe he was right in one sense. Maybe I was just seeking reassurance, but not simply because of my spell in prison. I wanted someone to tell me everything was going to work out fine. And most of all I wanted this man – with his well-muscled body and his sinewed arms tugging at the collar on the end of the hosepipe, his generous smile and easy manner of leadership – I wanted him to tell me that everything was going to work out fine.

My son is a good man, orang puteh. He is kind to his wife and children. He brings gifts to his father and his mother. He is good for the Company.

Gaing's father sat opposite me on a mat and rested against the wooden wall of a sleeping room in the longhouse. We were managing to maintain a faltering conversation in snatches of Malay and Murut, but mostly we were just sitting together as the after-dinner hubbub died down and the easy moves towards sleep took their course. Children who, after my second day, had grown accustomed to my whiteness and didn't come near me so much, were being led off to quiet corners by older brothers and sisters. Young women completed the cleaning and the men sat about talking to their children or each other in the half-light of candles and lamps. My head felt light and drowsy after the day's hunting. Mugang, Gaing's younger brother, had shot a forest deer and the whole longhouse had feasted. The cares and troubles of the timber camp seemed centuries away.

'How is your family these days?' I asked. Again Gaing's look was puzzled, so I hurried on to add, 'It was just… You mentioned the time I went to visit them with you last year. It seems so long ago.'

'Everyone is fine, I think. My brother, Mugang, passed through here yesterday on his way to the coast. He brought me news.'

Then I remembered seeing a man I knew wasn't one of our crew but who did look vaguely familiar. He had waved a greeting at me and I had replied absentmindedly. I really didn't know anything about the lives being led around me. I had only the vaguest of understandings of the trials and joys of the men I lived with. The men who walked for days to reach their home villages deeper in the hills, the men who had children at the secondary school at the coast, and who saw them three or four times a year as they passed through or when they managed to be home at the same time. And I realised that if I knew very little about the life of local men like Gaing, I knew nothing whatsoever about the real world of Ilpe and his fellow itinerant timber-camp workers from the Philippines.

'Do you ever get fed up with all this, Gaing? I mean, do you ever wish you were at home all the time?'

'Sure. But I have a family, you know. My boys are at the school.' He nodded his head in the direction of the coast. 'And I want them to get good jobs. Not like their father.'

My smile gave me away because he asked me, 'You think this is funny?'

'No, not funny at all. It is simply the sort of thing my father said about me growing up.'

And he smiled back at me in a way that made me feel connected for one fleeting moment to the myriad lives going on around me.

Then we heard a wild whooping noise backed up by the deep growling of a Mack coming to a swirling halt beside us. A ragged group of men passed chainsaws and shoulder bags to one another, shouting obscenities and light-hearted banter all the while. Ilpe leaned out of the cab and roared something which was drowned out by the dying grumble of the Mack's engine. He waved at Gaing and me, looked at the helicopter, hunched his shoulders, came over to us and beamed a smile. 'Looks like we got big-shot visitors. Must have bath then. All the men going to the river. You need a wash too. You look like a Mack shit on you.'

His infectious grinning easily won us over, and we just dropped our tools and our cleaning rags and ran after the shouting and laughing bunch of men, racing behind the cookhouse to where a makeshift beach had been cut away and filled with gravel so that we could play and wash in the river. Men stripped down to their shorts, some went in naked, and soon the stretch of river in front of us was alive with writhing, shouting timber-camp workers. I hesitated for a moment, when I noticed that the red weals seemed to have flared up on my shins once more. Do I have any of that cream left? I thought. But Ilpe was right behind me and he gave me a friendly shove as he roared past me.

'Get in, white man. You need to get rid of that prison smell too.' And with a wild 'Yee-haw' he splashed in among his colleagues and I lunged in after him.

There is a chastening awfulness about the river in flood. It has the colour of strong tea well milked, and it swirls as it would in a cup from which the spoon has just been lifted. I have often lain in its churning flow, my eyes facing upwards to the patchy sky backlighting the arch of trees and wondered to myself if it was all real. How did it come to pass that I could be in such a glorious place when all I ever did was get born in a small town in Ireland and go to college and make myself available for work? What mighty hand played a part in my coming to this?

All of a sudden, the chug-a-chug of the helicopter lifting off could be heard, and we all looked up to see the brightly coloured bird make its ungainly way out of the camp, hovering briefly above the cookhouse as if uncertain of its next move. Then, its confidence rising with the whine of its motors, it swivelled on an invisible axis and headed for the coast.

'Gaing says it means trouble.'

Ilpe was beside me, treading water, our faces inches apart.

'I don't know,' I replied.

'Maybe they want us to go back to prison,' he said, spluttering slightly. 'I mean me. Maybe they want me to go back to the prison. Or maybe they want to make Arkland go to the prison. Let him see how much he likes that shit.'

Then he swam away from me, powering out for the middle of the river where the current was strongest and where Gaing and a group of men balanced precariously on a fallen tree. From there they launched themselves into the tide and swam furiously towards the other bank, aiming for an overhanging branch. If you missed that, you weren't certain of making the bank without injury and ran the risk of being swept further downstream towards the rapids and falls that marked the beginning of the valley below us.

I swam after Ilpe and joined him balancing on the log in mid-stream. The swirl at our feet was awesome. Pieces of foliage raced by. The men tossed twigs into the flow, trying to gauge it. Suddenly Gaing launched himself against the tide, and for an awful moment I thought we'd lost him until his sleek black hair could be seen tossed about like a piece of flotsam on the water. His brown arms struck out awkwardly in front of him as he tried to steer himself across and against the current, aiming for the salvation of the overhanging branches. I shouted encouragement in English as the men laughed, cheered and jeered in their own languages. A mighty 'Hurrah' went up as his arm wrapped around a branch and he hauled himself out of the water to stand on the opposite bank, his shorts low around his thighs, where the water had pulled them, his shins scraped and red from the vegetation near the bank.

Now Ilpe took to the tide, and his progress across the raging water was as swift yet just as dangerous as Gaing's, but he had the benefit of Gaing being already there so that all he had to do was reach out an arm and he was hauled ashore. The two men waved back at us, then they hugged each other, the one light chocolate brown, the other darker but just as lithe.

Their embracing and waving seemed to present me with a challenge. I would have to make the swim. The other men on the log with me kept up a barrage of exhortation and advice, urging me to plunge in. I could feel the excitement of the dare rushing through me and though I knew it was madness, I braced myself to dive. I had crossed before but only during the dry season when the river was low and the current light. Then you just drifted calmly across, turning late on to gain the opposite bank. Now the river was in full flood. The water raced beside my feet and a great gulf of churning river lay between me and the far bank. As if to further heighten the dare, a great lump of tree came crashing by, twirling and bucking in the water, big enough to need two men to carry it, slapping about and heaving in angry battle with the surging current.

'Oh shit!' I roared and the men cheered as I launched myself into the river, immediately surfacing to feel the current slap me like a fist and tear at my legs, tossing me this way and that until I calmed myself and directed my energies into a bold hand-over-hand crawl against the rushing water, cutting across the current, giving me an angle to aim for, feeling the weight of water at my chest and the lean energy of my body knifing through its mass. The exhilaration made my heart beat faster, the massive surge of adrenaline made my muscles pump harder. My teeth gritted and I gulped air through my nose like a seal. I could see Ilpe and Gaing ahead of me, waving and leaning their hands out to me. I could see their lips move but heard nothing of their calls above the torrent of sound the water made in my ears. I seemed to be making steady progress towards them, but soon realised that I might not make it. How to judge these things? How do you know when to take the leap? When to reach out? When to make that final push?

You should have told me about it, Larry. You know we would have listened. You don't trust me, do you? Who do you trust, Larry? Yourself?

My father speaking to me from the depths of the river, coming upon me in my moment of distress, reaching out to me and yet not there. I gulped a mouthful and trod water, going with the current for an awful moment. I looked at the bank and saw that a boy stood between Gaing and Ilpe, tiny and quiet, staring with the mildest of looks on his face. And though I knew he was real and not the ghost of the Penan boy, but one of the kids from a nearby *kampung*, I lost all power from my limbs, as if I'd seen a ghost, and let the current's tentacles grip me hard.

'Get outa water, you motherfucker, Mahon.' Ilpe's voice, loaded with GI slang, carried over the torrent, and the will to life I thought was leaving me returned in a panic of adrenaline coursing through my body so that I began a fervent and frantic whimpering as I ploughed back against the current, making my body as streamlined and powerful as a salmon's, churning the current aside and striving, striving towards the bank.

'Your hand. Give us your hand.'

Ilpe's face was in front of me, and behind him I could see the prone figure of Gaing holding on to his leg. I grabbed the arm and held on tight. His fingers wrapped themselves round my forearm and squeezed like a vice. His grip said hang on or we'll both go down in this.

Other men used the rope bridge to cross the river, and joined Gaing, helping him to pull Ilpe and me out of the river, until we stood, lacerated and breathless, on the bank. My chest heaved as I gulped for air. Gaing slapped Ilpe on the back, and out of the corner of my eye I saw Arkland standing on the back step of the cookhouse. He raised his mug of coffee in salute, but it was the sardonic smile that told me he would just as easily have saluted my death by drowning.

CHAPTER TWELVE

'You trying to scare the shit out of us or what, white man?'

Ilpe joined Gaing and me in the cookhouse. I was recovering from my ordeal with a plate of Dapo's *nasi goreng*, rice fried in bush-pig fat with meat and vegetables scattered throughout, washed down with mugs of his strong gritty coffee.

'I never panicked. Everything under control,' I said.

Ilpe looked sideways at me, winked dramatically at Gaing, and pulled a cigarette out of the top pocket of his shirt. He had gone back to his room to change. He always looked his best, even after days of driving in the forest. 'Listen to you, man. Stuffing rice in your face like you didn't nearly drown only Gaing and me saved you. Well, next time you plan to take a long swim, just tell us and we'll wave you goodbye.'

There was a sneering smile on his face, with the merest hint of what I knew friendship could be about. He took a puff on his cigarette and continued, 'You know, Mahon, I have met white men like you before. Too long in the sun and your brain gets fried. I've seen good old boys from the USA go mad in the bars along Subic Bay, all because of some silly little misdemeanour they were supposed to have committed. You should have seen them when the MPs came. Shit scared.' He was using a cowboy drawl now, like a man in a film about himself. 'But you won't get someone like me going like that. You see, Mahon, our lives aren't as precious as yours. There's so many of us, for one thing, and we have so much hunger and disease that we don't have very high hopes of what's going down. You see, we're not white, and that's the bottom line. So we do our best with it and struggle on. Giving up is not a luxury we can afford.'

'I wasn't giving up. I just ran out of steam. Out of breath.'

'Same thing. Got to keep breathing all the time, even when your mouth feels full of shit and your belly is as empty as the ocean sky. Which it is now. Heh, Dapo?' He got up and went to the cooking corner and called to Dapo, who was sitting by the back door smoking a Marlboro.

I watched Ilpe from behind and wondered if he would ever respect me again. Had I lost face in some way? Would I ever know friendship from these men around me? The faces moving animatedly over plates of steaming *nasi goreng*. The smiles, often with missing teeth. The laughter and the quiet chat. The company of men, all of us far from home – even the locals had days to walk – joined in this singular enterprise to wrest the great trees from the earth and serve them up for disposal in Hong Kong and Japan, cheap as kindling.

Ilpe came back with a plate heaped high with fried rice, and two beers, opened.

'Here. Wash the dust out of your mouth, though maybe you swallowed enough of the river already.'

He let out a roar of a laugh and winked hugely at Gaing once more. Gaing winked back and said he had to leave, something about needing to sleep off the excitement. Ilpe started to wolf down his food. I took a slurp of the beer he had brought and tried the question in my head a few times before I finally asked it.

'Is there anything we can do about the boy?'

Ilpe kept on eating. Nothing in his actions or the way he bent over his plate indicated that he had even heard my question. He ploughed through the mound of fried rice, lifting off the slivers of golden-brown egg and the fatty pieces of left-over bush pig Dapo tossed into almost every dish, chasing the last few grains of rice around his plate, then belched loudly, pushed back on his chair and took a grand swig from his beer.

'There is nothing we can do for the boy. Like I said. We cannot afford the luxury of giving up. So if you want to worry yourself to death, go right on and do it. Just don't expect me to join you.'

'But don't you feel bad about it?'

'Don't be such a fuck-up, Mahon.' He leaned towards me,

pushing his face across the table. 'Course I feel bad about it. I've got kids myself back in Olangapo, don't I?'

'I never knew that. You never told me.'

'Yeah, that's right. Never needed to until now. But what you got to remember, Mahon, is that you're the company man and you're the white man, so if things get shitty it won't be you who goes down, it will be me. Not unless Arkland needs to save his own skin big time. Then my advice to you is watch your back.'

I nodded at Dapo and gave him the two fingers. The beers came almost immediately. Arkland and me were the only two men on the camp who could get waiter service like that. It seemed to confirm what Ilpe was saying.

'Where are your children now?' I asked.

'Back in the Philippines, living with my sister.'

'Their... mother?'

'Stateside!' he said with a silly grin. 'Living the American Dream. Least I hope she is. I just hope her life's better than the one she left to me and the kids.'

'I'm sorry...'

'Heh, Mr Mahon, don't get yourself worrying about it. You might try to drown yourself again!'

The grin widened across his face, but it couldn't hide the pain in his eyes brought up by this conversation. 'I don't blame her, you see. She did what she thought was best. Try to make a few dollars for the children. And if that meant selling her body, well, like I said, sometimes giving up is not a luxury we can afford, and the next step for her was to sell her soul. I hope she picked the right fella to go Stateside with. Funny thing about it. He was a friend of Arkland.'

Then he stood up and drained his bottle of beer. 'Just stay cool. Drink enough to get to sleep every night. And keep thinking about the nice white ladies and the nice white world you're going home to someday soon.'

*****

'We're getting a bit of heat here, Larry. First time I've really felt it like this. We're going to have to do something.'

Arkland was in my room. He'd come after my talk with Ilpe, just as I was about to start a letter to my mother. I had vowed on my return that I would write more regularly. I wanted news of Gerald and my father. Especially my father. But now, with Arkland pacing up and down the floor, I pushed my letter aside.

'You don't go in much for interior decor, do you?' he continued. The walls were bare except for a calendar of scenes from Ireland set one month behind. My camp bed was in the corner and the large crate I used for clothes was open, showing piles of shirts and shorts. The room was spartan but it was tidy and clean. Arkland's was a tip.

'What do you mean, heat?' I said.

'The guy who called today? You saw him? Air Force helicopter from Kuala Lumpur. That's heat. He's from the Ministry, right, and he says we've got to do something about it. The Minister is not happy. Not at all happy.'

'Not happy about what?' I wished he would sit down so I could get some sense out of him. 'Here, Greg. Here, take a seat. And start again.'

But he kept moving. 'And it's your fault, you know. Jesus, if you hadn't run over that kid, none of this would have happened.'

I suddenly felt cold, and shivered as if someone had walked over my grave. An image of Gerald in the dock flashed into my head, my face superimposed upon his. 'What about the boy? The police have dropped the case. No charges. That's what Merkat said.'

'Yeah. I know. But that was before the Minister got involved in it.'

'But how did he hear? And besides, if the police have dropped it, why should he be bothered?'

'Because of his daughter.'

'His daughter?'

If Arkland didn't sit down soon I was sure I would pull him

down. But he just kept pacing, lifting and dragging his bad leg, making a kalumping sound on the wooden floorboard.

'You remember the photographer in the forest?'

'Yes.'

'Datuk Pak Lee Chung's daughter.'

'Jesus.'

'Exactly. The Minister of Forestry's daughter is over here to protect the rainforest. Ironic, isn't it? Her dad can't get them chopped down fast enough. She's struck up with Penan near here. It was after the kid was killed. But she heard about it and told her old man. She says that if he doesn't shut us down she'll blow the story internationally – with photos. Datuk Pak Lee Chung and his boys at the Ministry are playing it cool for now. They're dealing with me direct and not telling anyone in Headquarters in Kuala Lumpur. They just want her back home fast.'

'But what can she do to us?' I was struggling to understand what all this meant.

'Jesus, Larry, it's on our patch. They're our Macks she's blocking with her gook friends. It was our jeep that you and that fuck Ilpe drove over the kid. And on my watch. If she... I'm going crazy trying to figure this out. If she gets killed or something over here, I'll never work again. And if they close this place down, no-one will take me on again. Never.'

Arkland finally sat down in the chair I had pulled up for him. He looked beaten and tired. He kept rubbing his bad leg, stuck out in front of him. Now I knew why he didn't care what happened to me when the police took me. He was busy trying to save his own skin, right from the very start.

He pulled his chair closer so that his bad leg almost touched my bare feet.

'Look,' he said. 'I didn't mean it when I said it was all your fault. If the whole damned thing is anybody's fault it's that fuck-up driver Ilpe's. He ran over the kid. That's what I said to the guy in the helicopter today. It's Ilpe we need to get. And if we do that, this eco-freak daughter of the Minister's will be happy and she'll go back to Daddy and there'll be no more talk of closing us down.'

114

'You've lost me, Greg,' I said, and I meant it.

'Jesus H Christ, Mahon. You dense or something? We can get Ilpe charged with killing the kid, that will pacify the daughter, and we can go on logging trees. And listen, I need your help in this.'

'I want no part of this.'

'Listen, Larry,' Arkland cajoled. 'We're in this together. Why, the police may come back for both you and Ilpe even now. I stalled the guy today when he suggested that. I said to leave you out of it. Took a bit of doing, but we're epiphytes, Larry, you and me, just like I said. So I told him we'd give them Ilpe. That you would testify that Ilpe drove on despite your order.'

In a way it had been like that. But I knew how far from the full truth that version was. I had run that scene through my head many times already, and I had pushed it away. But that was before I had spent my time in prison. I couldn't face that again. I kept seeing my father in front of me. I couldn't be in prison like Gerald. I couldn't have my father look at me the way he looked at me the night Gerald was lifted.

'What do you want me to do?' I asked.

'Nothing just yet. I'll take care of everything. Don't you worry, Larry me boy. Old Noah the Arkland will take care of everything, especially you, fellow epiphyte.'

He winked at me and left. I heard him drag his bad leg down the boardwalk and close his own door behind him with a resounding slam.

I hated him then. All my confusion and my uncertainties focused on him. I'd never felt like that before.

I returned to the letter to my mother. Try as I might, I couldn't keep my problems out of it. I gave her no details. Just an outline of problems with the concession and difficulties with my boss. I didn't mention the dead boy or the photographer. I asked about Gerald. Had they visited him? Could I write to him? What was happening to him? And I asked about my father, but I couldn't find words to express what I felt about him. I wanted to tell him it wasn't my fault that Gerald had been lifted. I had my own problems. I couldn't write anything like that. All I could manage was: 'Tell Da I was asking for him.'

Then I arranged the mosquito net around the bed, turned off the light and got under the sheet. The dull drone of the generator blocked out all the forest noises. Some geckos scampered on the walls, chasing and fighting each other, sometimes dropping their tails as their only defence. In the morning I would find them, if the ants hadn't carried them off.

Arkland's plan to save his skin was inextricably linked with my own problems. I couldn't go to prison, and so I would let Ilpe go. If that's what it took I would have to do it. Ilpe could drop off like a gecko's tail, and I would scamper to freedom. The Minister's daughter would go home and we would carry on logging as the Penan moved further into the forest. I tried to convince myself that's how it would be, and I was relieved when the generator's drone dulled my brain and I fell asleep.

CHAPTER THIRTEEN

To wake in the rainforest is to wake in paradise. I pushed open my wooden window as hornbills flashed brilliantly in the bushes beside me. There was a liquid-gold light among the trees and a party of gibbons was just moving out of sight, their rumps and curling tails the last I saw of them. I smelled the overnight rain soaking into the ground and the vegetable smell of the forest. I saw orchids, white and ruffed, high on a tree in front of me. Epiphytes, living on the fat of the forest. And I allowed all this to convince me that things were going to get better.

Dapo was frying pancakes in an oil made from bush-pig fat. I ate six of them and downed two mugs of the strong gritty coffee he kept brewing on the stove. The grader drivers came in and said they were ready. I pointed at my unfinished coffee and they grinned, poured themselves a mug each and lit up cigarettes. This was the way to start the day. A good breakfast and everything ready for work.

As I stepped out of the cookhouse, I saw the Penan group on the boardwalk in front of Arkland's office. Voices carried across the square to me and I heard Arkland talking in Malay. The grader drivers walked over to the vehicle compound, but I stepped back into the shadows of the cookhouse door.

'Everything is being dealt with, I promise you.' Arkland had broken into English, and when I saw the photographer on the edge of the group I understood why. 'The police investigation is coming to a close and they expect to arrest someone very soon. They have promised me this.'

Then he began to speak in Chinese, a pleading whine I'd never heard before in his voice. The photographer, now hidden from my view by the group of men, suddenly began to speak very fast Chinese. Arkland said something else and the group stepped off the boardwalk and walked away in single file. I stepped back further into the shadows, treading on Dapo's foot.

'Penan man not happy. Make trouble,' Dapo said.

The Penan group left the camp, entering the forest just behind the accommodation block. I waited for a long time before I left the cookhouse and went to Arkland's office. He was pacing around behind his desk.

'I'm just going to work on the road with a couple of graders,' I said, but it was as if I hadn't said anything.

'Did you see that bitch? Did you hear what she called me?'

'What are you talking about?'

'Ah, yes. You were probably still in your room beating your meat when I got a visit from the Minister's daughter and her trusty band of merry fucking men. And when I told her the cops were going to arrest someone soon, she said she hoped it would be me and any other *orang puteh* they could lay their hands on. Jesus. What a bitch!'

I knew it wasn't going to go as Arkland said it would. I knew that handing Ilpe over to the police would solve nothing, satisfy no-one, but it seemed as if that's what had to happen next. The wheels were in motion.

*****

I spent the day working with the graders. In slow, graceful sweeps, the wide blades levelled the surface of the road and lifted my heart. The humidity and the heat were awesome. The stench of the vehicle exhausts was terrible, the noise in my ears almost deafening, but I was glad of it all. At least I had other things to occupy my mind.

When I got back to the camp at sunset I was surprised to see groups of men standing around, talking in the square. They should have been bathing or in the bar, either way washing the day's work away. I got down off the grader I had ridden back on and went to wash my hands at the stand-pipe in the vehicle compound. The water was cold and silvery, and I let it play over my hands for a long time while glancing up at the groups of men standing talking. It seemed like everyone was there. The Filipino mechanics. The Murut chainsaw men. The Filipinos who drove the vehicles and did the other skilled work. Even Dapo was talking to the loggers on the step of the cookhouse. The grader drivers left the vehicle compound and joined a group.

Gaing came up to me at the stand-pipe. He waited until I had finished washing my hands, then he said, 'The police took Ilpe today.'

Though I knew this was coming, I was amazed at how fast events seemed to be moving. I said nothing. I just stood there gently shaking the water off my hands.

'They will charge him with killing the boy.'

I still said nothing, though the honest and open look on Gaing's face almost made me want to explain that I just couldn't do anything about it. I wanted to explain to him that the real reason was that my brother was in prison and my father somehow blamed me.

'You were in the Land Rover with him. You know what happened. It was an accident. We must go to the police and tell them this. We can go now, because tomorrow they take Ilpe to the capital.'

'I have told the police everything I know. I have no more to tell them.'

'But, for Ilpe. We must go down for him.'

'Speak to Arkland.'

'I did already. He says it is for the police. Arkland is no good. He doesn't care for anyone but himself and the concession. Somebody must go down. If the *orang puteh* goes down, maybe they won't go so hard on Ilpe. You must do it, Larry Mahon.'

'There is nothing I can do. Arkland is right. It is a matter for the police.'

Gaing looked at me briefly, then turned his head away and spat on the ground beside him. 'I am a fool. I thought you would be a friend to Ilpe. I was wrong. You are Arkland's friend, not Ilpe's. And not mine.'

Then he left me and walked to the cookhouse. When the men saw him they nudged each other, and in twos and threes they followed him into the cookhouse.

I stood in the vehicle compound in the fading light, my wet hands still dripping, a latter-day Pontius Pilate.

*****

'It'll blow over. A couple more days and it'll blow over. Besides, it gives us time to get this problem with the Minister's daughter sorted out. They'll forget Ilpe in a couple of days and we'll get back to business.'

We were in his office, in front of his beloved maps. I got the impression that Arkland was trying to convince himself as much as he was trying to explain things to me.

'I'm not so sure,' I said. 'The Murut men may go back to the villages. The heavy rains are coming anyway, so they know some of them would have been leaving. What's a week or two earlier to them? And the Filipinos. Maybe they'll leave for work somewhere else.'

'Jesus, you're being very helpful. No logging yesterday and that's the best you can offer.'

'I didn't hand Ilpe over to the police.'

'Not directly maybe. But you're up to your neck in it too, Larry Mahon. You want to save your skin too, my friend.'

I knew this was getting us nowhere. We had a strike on our hands and no way of dealing with it. Gaing wouldn't talk to us. The men simply refused to leave the camp. Some stayed in their bunks all day. Others, mainly the Murut, walked and hunted in the forest. Everyone was waiting for something. And that's all Arkland could suggest too. Just wait. I was getting scared of waiting.

'I think that if we wait around too long we'll have a riot on our hands,' I said.

'You think we should close down?'

'No, I don't think that. I don't know what to think.'

120

I had never before felt such exasperation. Would I crack? Ever since Ilpe had been arrested I had been feeling nothing but guilt. I didn't recognise it at first but it slowly dawned on me that I was now numb to every emotion except guilt and the fear that came with it. I was responsible for what happened to Ilpe. Just as I was responsible for what happened to the boy. And to my brother Gerald. This was the worst guilt. I should have been there, looking out for him. But that was something I felt I could do nothing about now, no matter what I heard my father say.

Ach, Larry. Take your wee brother wi' ya to the baths. Go on now. That's what big brothers are for. You can teach him to swim.

And more often that not I took Gerald with me, but I most keenly remembered the one or two occasions, no more than three, that I hadn't.

Arkland's voice finally drove out my father's.

'Yeah, a couple more days. We've got plenty of logs down for despatch. That gives us a couple more days. We'll just carry on as usual, you and me. Make like nothing's happening. Let them make the first move.'

Maybe he's right, I thought as I went back to my own office. Maybe a couple more days will do it and Ilpe will be forgotten about and we'll get on with business again. I had plenty of work to keep me at my desk until then. There was always a build-up of reports to file and projections to draw up.

I sat at my desk and looked out the window. Dapo was stirring a large pot of rice outside the cookhouse. Mealtimes were going to be hard. Arkland never seemed to eat, so it didn't matter to him. I had to have food. How could I sit in the cookhouse with all the other men and pretend nothing was happening? I would have to avoid the cookhouse. Maybe get Dapo to bring food to my room. It wouldn't be easy. It was how I imagined being under siege would be like.

*****

'Let's get out there and show these bastards that we won't be beaten.'

Arkland was standing outside my office early the next morning. I had been up for over an hour finalising a report before the heat of the day made office work unbearable. I could see him through the window and knew by his dress that he was ready for the forest. A baseball cap with 'Yankees' scripted in faded gold lettering was propped upon his head and he wore a T-shirt with ripped-off sleeves so that his sinewy upper arms bulged as he gestured to me.

'Get away from that desk, Mahon. We've got some surveying to do.'

I stood up and confirmed my impression that he was ready for action. He wore green army-fatigue trousers over large boots, with heavy socks bunched at the ankle to keep the leeches out. I went out onto the verandah and squinting at the sun, I asked, 'What do you have in mind? We can hardly log this forest ourselves.'

He leered up at me as if I was a child who didn't fully understand things, and as if his patience was running out with me. 'Look, you Irish fuck-up. Can't you see that we have to carry on as if nothing was happening? Like we're in control? So get your butt out of that office and into the Land Rover, and make like a surveyor, for Christ's sake.'

Five minutes later, we drove out of the camp. My surveying equipment lay bundled in the rear. The camp was eerily quiet, the men resting up in the unusual holiday. Leaving the place like that didn't seem like a way of exhibiting control. I wondered if it would be seen as flight. It was obvious Arkland didn't see it like that.

'Let them stew in it for a while. We can do a bit of an inspection. See how the road's coming along. Take a glance at the valley sector. Take in a few culverts, a couple of cuttings, a few stockpiles. Act like timber-men for once and not like some Johnny-jump-up office boys snowed under with reports and projections.'

Arkland drove like a novice, someone who'd never gotten past the idea that you just willed the vehicle to go where you wanted it to go and it did. It was as if he had never gotten used to the notion of coordinating his brain and his limbs to meld with the vehicle so that it would flow along. Within ten minutes, he was sweating heavily and swearing at every rut and turn.

'Goddam road, Mahon. You engineer this stretch of shit? Jesus!'

When we came to Kilometre Ten he stopped and got out. I followed him and stood in the middle of the road, looking for signs of the accident.

'Happened about here, didn't it?'

I said nothing, waiting to hear where this was all leading. Arkland walked to the edge of the road and looked over the valley below us. I stood well behind him and from my position it seemed as if Arkland had his head in the clouds.

'They're out there, you know. The Penan. Wandering around like some kind of lost tribe.' He picked up a clod of earth beside him and tossed it down into the valley. It was as if he hoped he might hit one of them.

'You got any tribes like that back in Ireland, Mahon, living in the forest, roaming about all over the place?'

I thought of the travellers who used to camp on the edge of my town, but I didn't think that's what he had in mind, so I said, 'No.'

'You're lucky then, aren't you?' And he tossed another clod of earth away from him. 'Come over here.' I went and stood beside him. We looked over the sea of green that stretched into the distance. I felt the heave of excitement such panoramic views of the rainforest always gave me.

'We're a pair of eagles, you and me, Mahon old pal. Lords of all we survey. The Penan and the Dayak may live among it, but we ride above it, confident and supreme. Basically we own it. They're like tenants. Pretty heavy stuff that, really. Big responsibility. That means we can't let ourselves get bogged down in trivia. Always got to keep the big picture in view. Focus on the main frame. Keep it in Cinemascope. Part of the white man's burden, eh? Ever since the white man came here all those years ago. And now we're the carriers of the torch, the keepers of the flame, the guardians of the grail... You still with me, Mahon?'

I nodded, though I really didn't have a clue what he was talking about.

'Now in the great way of the world, you've gotten yourself caught up in a minor hiccup. A slight problem has come up that I want to make sure doesn't tear you to pieces. Like, I'm your boss. More than a boss, really. More like friend. Or an older brother. Someone to guide you through the tough times. Like now.'

He bent down and lifted and tossed the third clod of earth.

'Thousands of species down there, Larry Mahon. All kinds of flora and fauna. No-one really knows just how much life there really is, teeming and fornicating and seething and growing. And dying and withering away. Your little Penan boy is just one dot in the mess of life going on in that forest. And you know something else? We're the only ones – us, the timber loggers – we're the only ones who have the guts to face it all. The only ones who have the guts to say, "Let's take it on. Let's put some light on the ground here. Let's make something of it." And if sometimes that means we've got to make a mess, so be it.'

I sort of knew what he meant. Something in the last-frontier feeling of his words echoed a part of my own reasons for joining Searwood. But I found he was making me nervous. I understood that he was trying to absolve me from any worries about the death of the boy, but I felt uneasy and my legs started to itch, so I reached down to scratch my shins.

'Jesus. What happened your leg?' Arkland asked.

'A bit of a rash. Doctor at home said it was nothing to worry about. He gave me some cream.'

'Did you get the rash back home?'

'No. I'm not sure really. Anyway, it's healing up okay.'

'Jesus. I hope so. Last thing we need is to have you medivacced out. Don't fancy being the last white man on the reservation, if you know what I mean.'

It was the first time I'd heard him acknowledge anything approaching fear. But even then he was smiling. 'We're frontiersmen here, Larry Mahon me boy. Rolling back the wilderness. Last outposts of civilisation, and our mission is to put some light on the ground in the face of this fecund darkness.'

His smile beamed at me and his face took on a vaguely evangelical brightness as if he was really moved by his rhetoric.

'Anyway. Enough of the sightseeing. Let's get back to the covered wagon over there and have a proper looksee at the logging site at Kilometre Twelve.'

My eyes followed his pointing finger toward the scar of fallen trees just below us. We could see the brown line of our road weaving down into the valley and then vanishing behind tormented piles of trees felled and discarded, which marked the limit of our logging at that point. The Macks had been due to go in, but that had been before Ilpe had been taken away.

Back in the Land Rover, Arkland continued to curse and swear as he drove, and I thought that the way he had to sit in order to get his shattered leg to reach the floor pedals must have had something to do with it. I found myself wondering what kind of pain he lived with, seeing him sitting half-turned away from me, his body thrown forward, as if grappling with the wheel.

We swung off the ridge and descended towards the valley. Soon we were in shadows as if we were entering a cavern. The great trees arched over us and Arkland had to turn on headlights to make sure we could see our way.

'Damned beautiful,' he hissed through his teeth, as if he found the place offensive.

We pulled up at Kilometre Twelve and got out to have a look. We walked down a short sloping track in the trees and came into the clearing that was our stockpiling area. All around us, felled trees lay against each other like giant matchsticks. And set apart in crudely ordered sectors were piles of rough logs, the newly cut and dragged-clear trees that had been stripped of branches and covering, and finally the piles of finished logs that would be hauled to the coast for onward shipping. I found myself blinking in the sunlight as I did some rough calculations of the amount of timber around us. Arkland walked over to a pile of finished logs and poked and sniffed them like a purchaser suspicious of second-hand goods. He was fired-up, pumping adrenaline, because he skipped to the top of the pile, dragging his bad leg behind him, to get an overview of our stockpiling.

'Looks good to me, Mahon. We're pulling some good stuff out of here. How long more you reckon we got here before we have to move on?'

'Hard to say,' I shouted up at him. There was no way I was going to climb up beside him. I'd seen too many log piles like that slither and crumble, squashing men underneath them like ants. 'I'll take a run further down in the next couple of days so we can be ready to move. I'll get the road in and prepare some projections.'

He seemed pleased enough, because he just nodded. Then he stood shielding his eyes and scanned the site, doing his own calculations. 'There seems to be a river over there. Let's take a look.'

Arkland jumped and bum-scraped down the pile of logs until he was beside me. It struck me that the exertion hadn't left him out of breath.

'You're in good shape, aren't you?' I said.

'If you ignore a leg with metal fatigue, yeah, I'm in good shape.'

He was grinning at me as we moved across the site and re-entered the trees. My eyes adjusted to the dim light once more. A grey-green dullness was interspersed with brilliant shafts of golden light where the top layers swayed apart to allow sunlight through. It always reminded me of being under the sea. And even now I could hear water rushing above the sounds of trees swishing overhead and the calling of birds and insects. There were no paths here and every now and then Arkland used the parang he had brought from the Land Rover to clear a way over the vines and roots that wove and coiled underfoot. Mostly we clambered around the great buttressed sides of the big trees, often losing our footing on the exposed roots that boiled and frothed from just below the surface of the soil.

The sound of water became louder, and we came to a rocky out-cropping that gave us a view of a pool and a swirling stream running away from us further down the valley floor. I was so enchanted by the darkness of the pool and the rush of the water that I didn't immediately see the Penan group on the far bank. I spotted the baby first, being swiftly swung onto the mother's back. An older girl lifted a basket and put it on her own back, placing the forehead strap across her brow in an unhurried movement. There was no panic. It was as if they were about to leave anyway. A man rose from where he had been resting on his haunches and gathered something into a pouch he swung across his shoulder. Two small fish were tied to a frond around his waist. I saw the earplates inserted into the lobes of his ears and felt how alien we were to each other. And yet when I looked again I saw he must be about my age and there he was with his own family, a woman to love and children to cherish, and I envied him bitterly.

'What makes them come so close to our stockpile?' was the only thing Arkland wanted to know. 'How come they know there's no logging going on today?' But before he could attempt to find out, the Penan family moved off, slowly and quietly, the woman carrying the baby and the man guiding the girl with the basket on her back up the side of the stream.

'Gooks. They're all the fucking same.' Arkland spat after them. 'Same all over the place. Nam. Here. Never met a good one yet. Even the ones supposed to be fighting with us just couldn't wait to get our backs turned before knifing us. Never knew where you stood with them. Couldn't trust them. It's worse than that here. Least in Nam we could go in there and blow them away. Here, we've got to go softly-softly and hope they don't create too much of a stink. But you see, Mahon, if these blockades start to heat up, I'm not to going to wait around for no lily-livered gook cop to come and sort it out. I can do that myself.'

He turned and clumped down off the rocks and back towards the clearing where our logs lay scattered. I stood for a few more minutes listening to the water, absorbed in the coolness of the forest, deeply concerned that I should be envious of a forest-dweller.

By the time I got back to the Land Rover, Arkland had the tailgate down and was sitting in the back with his boots off. 'I don't know which are worse. The gooks or the leeches.' Despite his arrangement of boots and heavy socks, a number of leeches had made it onto his feet and he was prying them off with a twig.

'The leech is a blood-sucking annelid worm, did you know that, Mahon? That means it's made up of rings and it sucks your blood. Now if I was a religious man, I would have to say that the leech is the good Lord's one mistake. All you can do with them is pick them off and flip them away.'

He had managed to prise one free from between his smallest two toes. He held it aloft for a moment on the end of the twig and then flipped it into the trees beside us. 'But see, if you do that they only come back. Sometimes you have to do something final with them.'

This time he managed to get hold of one between his thumb and finger. He peered closely at the engorged red blob.

'Amazing. This bastard has been sucking away at my blood as I've been walking around here. Jesus, doesn't it get you down sometimes?'

The leech dropped out of his hand and landed on the bed of the Land Rover beside him. Arkland picked up his boot and brought it down on the worm with a crisp smack. When he lifted the boot, the red sludge of the worm and his blood lay like the droppings of some mythical bird.

'Sometimes that's the only thing to do. Only problem is, there's not enough time for all the leeches. Or all the gooks for that matter. Have to pick and choose, unfortunately. Let's hope we've picked a good one in Ilpe.'

He checked his feet again and having satisfied himself that they were leech-free, he put his socks and boots back on.

'Time to return to base. See what they're up to. You drive this time. I want to sit out back for a while. And drive carefully.'

He pulled the tailgate back up as I went into the cab. All the talk of leeches made me feel as if the insides of my own boots were alive with them, squirming and sucking. But I resisted the desire to check my feet, using all my engineer's rationality to convince myself that the boots I used were specially designed to keep them out, and that I had been in the forest for only a short time anyway. I just sat in the cab feeling the unease between my toes climb up my shins so that, eventually, I had to reach down and scratch my rash before I could feel comfortable enough to drive off.

We made it back to the main road and turned for the camp. I was conscious of Arkland in the back of the Land Rover. I kept glancing at him in the rear view mirror. He lay in the body of the vehicle, in a corner between the side and the tailgate, his legs stuck out in a V in front of him and his brawny arm resting on the side wall. He seemed like a lord running his eyes over his domain. I felt like a vassal willing him to be happy, trying not to draw his attention onto me too much, striving to be invisible.

The drive was uneventful until at about Kilometre Ten, when Arkland suddenly lurched upright and bounded towards the cab. I saw his figure loom large in the mirror and then I heard him thump on the roof of the cab. His head appeared in the window beside me and I had a close-up of the leathery skin of his face as he shouted, 'Pull over. Gooks. Bastards are stalking us.'

I stopped the Land Rover and got out. Arkland had jumped down and was standing in the middle of the road, hands on hips, staring into the trees.

'Bastards are watching us. Been following us since we came onto the road here. Bold as brass too, letting us see they're here.'

He spoke in a tense whisper and I followed his gaze to look at the trees. Like pillars in a vaulted cathedral, they ranged away from me, light playing fitfully among them, the ticking of the Land Rover engine as it cooled, beating against the continuous humming of the birds and insects in the forest. We got out and stood side by side, staring into the forest. I saw nothing unusual until Arkland dramatically raised his arm and pointed to a large meranti slightly to our left. Standing beside the buttressed roots were two Penan men. Other figures seemed to be behind them, but it was hard to tell.

'Trying to psyche us out, they are. Gooks always try to do that. Part of their technique.'

His whole attitude was alarming. He seemed to be in battle readiness. His muscles were all tense. His jaw was clamped as he snarled the words out. I expected him to swing a machine gun from his side and go blazing into the bush. He might jump into the Land Rover any minute and grab the radio to put through a call for reinforcements or to bring in air cover. Get the napalm up here, Jody. Some gooks needing roasting. Over.

He kept staring at the figures in the woods and snarled at them, 'Come on then. Think you can just shadow me like that? I know your type. Been up your asses before. You don't scare me one bit. Get it?'

Then there was a flash of light and a rustle of undergrowth as a figure moved from somewhere further to our left and joined the men we could see. Arkland leaned forward as if he was going to run at them, but with simple calm movements they backed away and then turned and were lost to view in the great dark of the forest.

'They're nothing but shadows. Not human. And you know the best way to get rid of shadows, Mahon? Get them out in the sunlight. Put some light on the ground. That's what we're doing. Putting light on the ground. Getting rid of the shadows.'

And he went back to the Land Rover, swinging his bad leg in an ungainly arc over the tailgate. I stood for a moment longer trying to make out the figures in the forest, feeling suddenly cold and scared. Did I want to be part of Arkland's war?

'You going to stand there all day?'

Arkland's shout made me turn back to the vehicle. I restarted it and continued the journey back to the camp. As we breasted the final rise just before the camp entrance, I looked out of the left-hand window. I could see out over the valley, where the sea of tree-tops extended into the far distance. On the horizon, the rolling peaks of the next range rode that sea like great sea lions nonchalantly basking in the sun. The sight always made me catch my breath, and on that day I gasped out loud, realising that if Arkland was right, we were going to put some light on the ground but somehow make everything more dark.

CHAPTER FOURTEEN

The atmosphere at the camp remained tense. There was a standoff. It really was like being under siege. Arkland stayed in his office. I stayed in mine. Neither of us went to the cookhouse. Groups of men moved about the square in the middle of the camp. Or lounged on the verandah of the cookhouse or in the shade of the high sides of the Macks in the vehicle stockade. I saw Gaing once or twice in the distance but didn't try to approach him. It was too early in the standoff for that.

In the evening I went to my room, shouting to Dapo, standing alone on the steps of the cookhouse, to bring me some food after sunset. I threw off my clothes and stood in a sarong, trying to ease the tensions out of my shoulders as I ran my mind over Arkland's behaviour in the forest, where I had somehow become caught up in his re-enactment of his Vietnam days. It made me smile until Gerald came to mind and I had to acknowledge that my brother was a soldier too, and if I didn't know how he thought, how could I possibly figure out what to make of Arkland's meanderings?

I went outside to my backyard, stepped out of my sarong and sloshed water over myself, soaping all over in the way I'd learned from the local men. Then I poured two buckets over myself to rinse the soap off. The chill of the water was so refreshing that for those brief moments I was cleansed of all worry. Pleasant thoughts of dancing with Bronagh McCann at the wedding came to me, reminding me of the sway of bodies and the jolly crush of people. It made me softly nostalgic for home. It amused me to think that I could feel like that. A natural sort of feeling for someone overseas like me. An ex-pat doing his bit in the wide world of commerce and trade.

Back inside I rubbed myself down. If I wasn't fighting a war, what was I doing? I was wise enough to know that there is always an amount of 'running away' involved in any 'going to' something. And the events at home left me in no doubt that part of the reason I was in the rainforest was because I didn't want to be at home.

A thump on the wooden boardwalk and a muffled shout made me wrap my towel around me and open the door in time to see Dapo's back crossing the compound to the cookhouse. On the boards in front of me he had left a covered plate of food, a jug of coffee with a mug dangling on its edge, and a tin mug of water. This was his way of maintaining the stand off. He would serve Arkland and me, but he didn't have to talk to us if he didn't want to.

I took the food inside and got dressed. I sat down and ate with great pleasure. I guessed that being able to eat the local food in the remote locations I found myself was a bonus. I loved the heaped plates of rice, steaming and dirty-white. I wolfed down the chicken stews that were our staple, being one of the few dishes you could safely expect Dapo to produce. And Dapo knew I loved the tangy taste of the fried fern leaves known as *pakis*, so he made sure I always got some.

Belching grandly after the meal, I took a swig on the mug of water, saying out loud, 'Whatever about my reasons for coming here, it's Dapo's cooking that keeps me here.'

I took the mug of coffee out to the verandah and set it on the ground. Then I went back inside and brought out a chair. I sat with my legs propped on the verandah railings drinking coffee and looking up at the hundreds of stars scattered across the pure black sky like tiny shards of glass.

'That's what keeps me here,' I said softly to myself as I languished in the warmth of the evening, sensing the crowd of men eating in the cookhouse by the smell of the cooking fires and the gentle hum and clatter that crossed the compound to me.

Another scene of people eating came to me. There was a man, his great round earlobes flashing in the light of the fire. He was skinning two fish, tossing the entrails to a scrawny dog beside him. A woman was laying leaves on flat rocks. She had plaited strong twigs together and now the man was putting the fish across this grill, dusting the opened fillets with salt. He held the grill in one hand, gently tossing the fish to keep it from sticking. The woman crossed behind the fire and passed some sago meat, the rich inner paste of the sago palm, to the baby who sat with the older girl.

The girl helped the baby put the food into its mouth and both mother and daughter could be seen talking gently to the baby, coaxing it with smiles and grins. The man looked up from his cooking every now and then. He looked across at the rest of the family, tossing the fish on the hand-held grill, holding it just out of the range of the flickering flames, smiling to himself as he called across and the others turned to him, wide smiles lighting their faces, the glow from the fire making them seem golden and magical.

Low murmurings drew my reverie beyond this first family, to see just behind them, other domestic gatherings, men, women and children, seated around fires in comfortable groups. Two old women were plaiting the hair of young girls. A man used a leaf to play peek-a-boo with a baby. Two young women sat side by side in earnest conversation. Friends, I supposed, discussing love perhaps.

And in the full light of one of the main cooking fires I saw the photographer. She had her cameras and her bags laid out on a rattan mat. She held rolls of film, putting some of them in little black containers, slipping small bags of silica gel into the canisters and sealing them. She worked methodically and precisely, her equipment ranged before her in an orderly fashion. She was frowning in concentration, her shoulder-length black hair pushed back over each ear. Then she picked up a notebook covered in a plastic cover and made notes. Dates, locations, times, subjects. I saw my name. And Arkland's. We were in her book. Fully known to her. I was impressed by her professional and detached manner. Totally absorbed in her work. Single-minded. The light from the fire matched by the light in her eyes as she documented what Arkland and I were doing.

The reverie began to break up and the photographer was wearing a blue bridesmaid's dress, and she looked up at me smiling so that I mouthed her name, Bronagh, as the sound of men clumping down the steps of the cookhouse told me that mealtime was over and I came back to reality, picking up and drinking the last dregs of my coffee.

The men gathered in groups of three or four. Small flashes of light like fireflies showed them lighting up cigarettes. Softly billowing smoke above their heads confirmed the stillness of the night. I sighed in relief and relaxation. Pushing my feet against the railing and leaning back in my chair, I relished the last taste of coffee and wallowed in the afterglow of my reverie. I vowed silently not to analyse it too much. Just let it happen. Ease up on being the engineer for once. Just enjoy it rather than trying to figure it out. I was killing myself trying to figure things out. There was nothing I could do about so much of it all. Bronagh. The photographer. My father. My mother. Gerald in prison.

Jesus. The very thought of it made me shiver, thinking of the gecko's frantic running, my own tears. At least Gerald will have his comrades. Where were mine, especially now, with Arkland and me totally isolated from the men? We couldn't even eat with them.

There was a guffaw and a loud roar as two men came out of the cookhouse together. All the other men turned their heads to see them. I could see their outlines, but it wasn't clear who they were. One stood with his head bowed and his shoulders hunched. The other seemed to tower over him while he shouted and gesticulated. I was too far away to make out what was being said, but it looked fairly serious. I could see a group of men gathering behind them just inside the cookhouse, but the two men arguing continued to block the doorway.

The taller man raised himself to his full height and yelled something at the other man, wagging his finger and sticking his neck out. Then he turned to walk away towards the front of the boardwalk. The smaller man stepped forward and touched him lightly on the shoulder, which made him half turn backwards. Then the smaller man took a step back and to the side, crouched and bunched himself into a ball before launching a right uppercut, catapulting himself like a shotput thrower upwards behind his bunched fist into the jaw of the bigger man. The blow lifted the man two feet off the ground and he fell like a great tree onto the boardwalk.

The men who had been blocked inside the doorway now spilled out, and I recognised Gaing. He stood as if centre stage, and I admired his ease as he nodded to some men nearby who quietly but firmly stood in front of the fallen man as he got to his feet. They slowly moved him to the end of the boardwalk. He was offered a cigarette and a chance to tell his story.

While looking after this group, Gaing kept a tight grip on the arm of the other fighter as he was quietly surrounded by more men. It was like watching a play. Something was being staged for my benefit. An action piece to highlight the violence and camaraderie that made up our world. The world that really existed in the camp, the world Arkland and I could only observe from the wings, coming on as bit players every now and then.

The punch-thrower said something and there was a ripple of laughter. Dapo appeared with a length of cloth and the man's hand was bandaged. The group further along the verandah cautiously moved back to the centre and the men stood around, allowing the two fighters to see each other from a safe distance. Another peal of laughter rang out, more general and livelier than the first. Gaing said something, swivelling his head from side to side, talking to the two men, giving them a lecture. A friendly warning. A dressing-down. He pointed across the compound at Arkland's office as he spoke, and there were murmurings of agreement.

I picked up my coffee cup and went back into my room, glad to be out of the view of the men and conscious that this spartan space was my only real refuge. Reveries alone wouldn't help me.

*****

The next day I decided to make a trip to town to send some cables to head office. The atmosphere was growing more and more tense. Arkland didn't seem to notice.

'Good idea, Larry. I've a couple you could take and send for me. Check the mail while you're down there. Good idea.'

He was fiddling with his beloved maps, shifting pins and checking road plans I had drawn up. He was behaving as if nothing was going on.

I drove out of the vehicle stockade. Every other vehicle was in place. For the third morning, nothing had left the camp. It looked like all the men were still in their bunks, though they would usually have been in the forest two hours by that time.

It was downhill all the way to the town, with glimpses of the sea every now and then. The forest had been logged in this area and secondary growth dominated. It didn't have the majesty of the primary forest but it was still impressive. And the sun shone, as it did most mornings. The afternoons were almost all given over to the rains now. And I knew more and more would come. If they were heavy enough, they might save us, because we could close the concession.

But now the sun shone as I drove into the small coastal town near the camp. I shivered when I passed the police station, remembering my time there. I drove to the post office, where we had a box and from where we could send cables, past the row of eight shops on a raised verandah, facing the sea. It was quiet and slow and peaceful, and I was relieved to get out of the camp. I sent the cables and asked for the camp's mail. There were a couple of letters and newspapers for Arkland from head office, and a personal letter for me. The writing on the envelope was familiar, but I didn't fully recognise it. The postmark was Derry but I had no idea who had sent it to me. When I opened it and saw it was from my father, I let out a gasp that made the postmaster look up from his work.

I went round to Fat Cheng's *kedai* and ordered coffee. I had to push a pile of mah-jong blocks to one side to make room on the table. When the coffee came, I reopened my father's letter.

He had never written to me before, not when I was at college in Belfast or since I'd been overseas in the rainforests.

Dear Lawrence,

I am writing to give you the news from home. I am not the best man for writing letters but here goes anyway.

Your brother is on remand. He is up again in a couple of months' time. They'll probably put his case back again. That's what they usually do. He's keeping well anyway. His spirits are fine. When I told him I was writing to you he said to say he was asking for you. If you want to write to him, just send me the letters and I'll send them on.

I suppose you're surprised that I'm writing to you. Your mother is the one who usually does all that. Well, Larry, I have to tell you she's not well. Nothing serious. Her nerves, the doctor said. She took bad a few days after Gerald was lifted. And she kept saying to herself that she had to write to you and she's in no fit state to do that, so I said I would do it.

I got work on the new houses in Foyle Springs so that's good. Mrs Heaney drops in to keep an eye on your mother for me. Derry City are still top of the table. They should win the League now. And the Cup too! But you were more of a swimmer. It was Gerald who liked the football.

Well, Larry, I'd better pack it in now so I can post it this afternoon. Your mother will be onto me if I don't.

Write to her when you get a chance. She'd love to hear from you.

All the best,
Dad

I was glad I was alone in the *kedai*, because I began to cry. Slow silent tears started to fall, rolling down my cheeks onto the table. I was sad and angry that he didn't ask me to write to him. But why should he? We had no relationship. He was writing for my mother, not for himself. And yet I could use this terse and stilted letter as an excuse to write to him.

The click of a camera made me look up to see the photographer standing on the verandah just outside the *kedai*. She had just taken my photograph and was turning to walk away. I sprang from my seat and followed her.

'Who do you think you are, taking my photograph like that?'

She ignored me and walked along the verandah in front of the shops. I grabbed her arm outside the provisions shop just as she reached the open sacks of rice at the entrance.

'You're just a spoiled little rich girl playing at things you don't understand. You have no right to take my photograph like that.'

'You have no right to grab my arm like this,' she said and shook herself free. She was taller than I had thought and brown enough to be Malay. I was surprised to find her pretty. Her eyes were very bright, as if they were laughing.

'Go back where you came from. You're just making trouble around here,' I said.

She laughed. A rich strong laugh that creased up her eyes and showed her fine white teeth. 'You go back where you came from, *orang puteh*,' she said. 'At least this is my country.'

She turned and walked away from me. I would have followed her, but I saw two or three Penan men at the end of the verandah, so I went back to Fat Cheng's. My palms were wet and sticky. I knew my face was flushed. I shouldn't have spoken to her. I had made a fool of myself. I nearly always did where women were concerned.

*****

Arkland was pouring me a second large measure of Jack Daniels when he said, 'Have you seen your picture in the newspaper?'

'What?'

He tossed me the newspaper I had brought to him from the mailbox. It was a copy of *The New Straits Times*, a few days old. 'Check out page three. I have a friend who keeps an eye on stories that might interest me and sends them on to me.'

Arkland and I stared out of separate photos from a story entitled 'Borneo Forest Murder Cover-Up'. The story ran to three columns and the photos showed me, with survey markers in my hand, and Arkland, head only, wearing his soiled headband.

'They're her pictures,' I said.

'And her story, you can bet too,' said Arkland. 'There's nothing in it, but it doesn't do me much good to have my picture all over the papers. I can expect someone from HQ to contact me now. She's ballsed it up for me good and simple.'

I wasn't really listening to him. My eyes had immediately focused on my name in the story:

> The Land Rover which killed the child was driven by a
> timber-camp worker, possibly the engineer at the
> camp, Lawrence Mahon. Unconfirmed reports say that
> he and a Filipino assistant were in the forest surveying
> for new forest roads on the day the boy was killed.

'It was a waste of time handing over Ilpe. Even if she goes back to her daddy now, the damage is done. HQ will be onto me and I'll be for the chop.' Arkland laughed. A deadpan hollow laugh that drew my attention away from the newspaper.

'What do you think will happen now?'

'They'll try to screw me. I know that. They'll try to pin everything on me now. And if they come now, with everyone on strike, I'll really be done for. First thing to do is get the men back to work. Do a deal with them. Got to get them back to work immediately. And you, Larry me boy, you're the man to do it.'

We were in his room. The walls were bare with nothing to break the rough surface of the wood panels except a standard-issue photograph showing him in a formal military uniform as if he was receiving a medal. I'd known him over a year and it was in the weeks since the boy was killed that I had really learned how self-centred he was. Now I heard him trying to embroil me further in his plans.

'Look, Larry, you can't sit there all night staring at your picture in the paper. I've been thinking that maybe you'd be better off if Ilpe was out. Either way, he's no threat to me. But he might just start talking and if they pin a murder on him, the bastard might make you an accomplice.'

There was a definite smile on his face. He had me trapped. I couldn't tell if he had worked all of it out in advance or if he was reacting to things as they arose, but he mistook my emotion.

'Don't chicken out on me now, Larry! What we've got to do is keep the concession open at all costs. And that means getting those gook fuckers,' he nodded towards the compound, 'logging again. And pronto. Talk to Gaing.'

I must have given him what he took to be some sign of agreement, because his smile widened and he came at me with the bottle of Jack Daniels.

'Here you go, Larry me boy. Don't look so down. We'll work it out, no sweat. But you've been down ever since you got back from leave. Everything all right at home? Nothing wrong back there that's bugging you?'

I knew he couldn't really be interested. Couldn't care a damn about me or my family. I knew all this and yet his words offered the first opportunity to unburden myself of all the emotions I was feeling since my trip home.

'I don't know,' I said. 'There's just a lot of things going on at home now.'

'Everyone okay? Someone sick or something?'

'My mother apparently. I got a letter from my father today. You know, I can't remember him ever writing to me before. Crazy, isn't it? He says my mother is sick. That's the only reason he wrote. He says she can't but that she wants to. So he did instead.'

'What's she got? Your mother.'

There was something blocking me from telling him about

my mother's sickness. I would have to tell him about Gerald if I did that and I realised I was ashamed of having a brother in prison. This shocked me and made me feel angry. Why shouldn't I tell Arkland? I thought. Or anyone else for that matter.

'My brother was arrested when I was at home. My mother's been in shock since. She'll be on tranquillisers. Only half with it. She'll be okay, I suppose, when the sentence is known. The uncertainty will be over then.'

'What did he do?'

'He may have blown someone up.'

'Jesus. He's in the IRA?'

'Looks like it. I still can't believe it myself. We're not even a Republican family. Not as far as I know anyway.'

'Here.' Arkland poured more Jack Daniels into my glass. 'One for the road. We'd better not make it a long night. We could have the men back in the forest tomorrow. Get an early conversation with Gaing and get to the police station as soon as you can.'

He sat down and propped his bad leg on a section of meranti branch he used as a footstool. He swirled the bourbon in his glass and became lost in his own concerns. He'd done with me and was confident I would do as he said. His concern for my family had been small talk, a light diversion. I regretted I had told him about Gerald. I wasn't ashamed about it any more. I just knew it gave Arkland more power over me to know that Gerald was in prison.

*****

Dapo brought coffee and fried rice to my office the next morning, the arrangement I had made since the strike had begun. I told him to ask Gaing to come to see me.

I hadn't worked out what I was going to say, so that when Gaing came I panicked. 'Look, Gaing,' I said. 'There is no way this can go on. We've got to get the men back to work.'

He almost laughed at me. I could see the laughter welling up in his eyes, but it didn't sparkle there. It clung to his flat face as a mocking grin. 'The men will go back to work when I say so.'

I had to do something to recover the bad start I'd made. I didn't want to be fighting with this man. We could have been friends. I prided myself on always being good with the local people, wherever I was. It was Arkland who had the problems in that direction. I felt I was doing his dirty work for him again. And as long as I needed to save my own skin, he would be able to make me do that. I tried to make a fresh start with Gaing.

'Look, I made a mistake. A big mistake. I should have gone after Ilpe. You said so yourself. Well, it was just that Arkland told me not to. Ordered me not to. You know what he's like.' The lie came easily. I was becoming good at it. 'But I've just spent two days arguing with him about it,' I continued. 'And I'm going down right now to get Ilpe out.'

Gaing knew I was lying. I saw the mocking grin change to a look of pity and disbelief, but I was tied to Arkland's shifting plans. It didn't matter if Gaing pitied me as a weak and foolish man.

'Arkland said he would sack me if I went after Ilpe. I said that apart from it being the right thing to do, it was the only way to get the logging started again. That made him rethink and he said to me that if I got the logging started again, I could go down to get Ilpe. So, I'm asking you to help me. Talk to the men. Get them back into the forest. And I will go to the police station and get Ilpe.'

The mocking disbelief disappeared from Gaing's face. I had convinced him. I knew that even before he spoke. Yet, instead of elation, I felt bitterness and defeat.

'I will talk to the men. They will go back to work. They need the concession too, even more than Arkland or you or the company. You get Ilpe.'

He got up immediately and left my office. I saw him cross the square to the cookhouse. He entered and almost immediately Dapo came out and beat the oildrum he used to call mealtime. It was just after ten o'clock in the morning, and in the pattern of the past few days, the men had either gone back to their bunks or were lounging in small groups in the

143

shade. Now they went in twos and threes to the cookhouse. The small, squat Murut loggers, kinspeople of Gaing. The dark-skinned Filipino drivers, hardened by years in the timber camps in the Philippines, Indonesia and Malaysia.

I watched them all enter the cookhouse and in less than five minutes they came out again, some smiling, all eager and more alive. The loggers got their chainsaws. Some had hard hats. They climbed into the backs of the already running Macks. And in a small convoy they headed out of the camp, hours late but going to work for the first time in days. Then two graders, more stately than the trucks, processed from the camp. Gaing and a fellow mechanic set to work in the vehicle stockade.

Dapo came to the door of the cookhouse and surveyed the quietened compound. He rubbed his palms together in the universal gesture of pleasure and energy, and went back into the cookhouse.

I got up from behind my desk and walked out to the Land Rover. I was convinced that I had no control over what was happening, but the pattern was so set now that I had to carry on. I saw Arkland at his window as I turned the Land Rover. He gave me a curt wave, his best wishes. After all, I was his puppet. Why shouldn't he wish me well?

CHAPTER FIFTEEN

'Mr Mahon. You have come back to us. You must have enjoyed your last visit.'

Sergeant Merkat's irony was lost on me. I was too busy reliving memories of my time in the police cell. Two days of unremitting terror that I would have raised hell about at consular level except that I didn't want anybody to look too closely at the affair.

'I just want to see Ilpe. The driver,' I said.

'Aah yes. The Filipino.'

Merkat made it sound like Ilpe was being held for a minor offence, as if he were one of many petty criminals he had in custody at that time. He shuffled some papers on his desk and then stood up, taking an official letter with him to the window. Like most buildings in the village, the police station was raised on stilts. There was a view of casuarina trees and the South China Sea beyond.

'You know, Mr Mahon, in our history, pirates used to sail these seas, all the way past Kudat and on to Mindanao. Your friend Ilpe may have had ancestors among them. Then your ancestors came, Mr Mahon, and piracy became a very different profession. Aah yes. I often yearn for simpler days. You see, I've just received this letter advising me to release the Filipino immediately.'

'So he'll be released?' I blurted.

'Of that I am sure, Mr Mahon. But not by me.'

'I don't understand.'

'Your friend Ilpe is not with us but is in the capital. We sent him there. We thought it would be safer for him. The Penan, you know, might have attacked the police station.'

'So you will be contacting your colleagues in the capital?'

'Of course. But they may also have received a letter. That is a possibility from the way in which the Minister's permanent secretary has written here. It is curious that the Ministry of Forestry would be concerned with a Filipino driver in this way. And to be so remarkably well informed about the case. It is a very interesting document, this letter. It is one I shall treasure, I assure you.'

He was smiling as he walked back from the window, holding the letter in front of him. 'Sit down, Mr Mahon. I have been impolite. I have not been hospitable.'

'That's all right. I think I'll leave if you don't mind. So, Ilpe will be released. You're sure of that?'

'You have my word.' And waving the letter, 'Or rather you have the Minister's word.'

I left Merkat and the police station then. I stood in the sun for a few minutes to let the chill seep from my bones. I knew I would never be able to go into a police station again without reliving the pain of my own time there. Or without thinking of my brother Gerald locked up somewhere.

*****

So things got back to normal at the camp. We logged the furthest reaches of the hills to the north of us, stripped and trimmed the logs, hauled them to the river and floated them out to the waiting ships which took them to Korea and Japan. The monsoon was slow in arriving and we were making reasonable progress. Nonetheless, we would soon have to decide to move camp to push further upland, or change direction and go down into the valley for logs.

My days took on their old rhythm once more. Most mornings I rose early with the men and left with them into the forest. I was keeping roads open, checking on the vehicles, monitoring tree cover. Other days I would stay in my office working on reports or analyses, keeping the paperwork in order. Arkland was preparing a quarterly summary, a task which kept him trapped at his desk, in foul temper. I passed data to him and otherwise kept myself to myself. It was a relief to be able to give my thoughts solely to work. I loved the return of normality.

But things couldn't go on like that indefinitely. I knew we'd have to move somewhere soon. Production figures for the quarter Arkland was reporting on would be down, but that could be covered by reference to the early monsoon rains. But I had to have projections for the next quarter's production. That meant deciding where we were going next. The most obvious place was down into the valley. I would have to survey it, mark it out for access roads and get the loggers in there. When I spoke to Arkland about this, he dismissed me.

'Leave it to me, Larry, will ya? I know what I'm doing here. There's plenty of logs up there for now.'

'But what about the projections? What about the next quarter?'

'Will you never lay off?' he roared. 'Just keep logging up there and leave the projections to me. Looking at things now, there may be no concession here next quarter.'

Arkland was keeping things from me. I was sure of it. There were papers on his desk from the office in Kuala Lumpur. And scattered sheets of paper in his cramped handwriting. He must have been composing his version of the newspaper story. I was certain he was doing all in his power to save his job, up to and including ditching me, or anyone else for that matter.

I left him and decided to concentrate on the work in hand, as well as on trying to figure out ways of protecting myself. I would need friends and I sought out Gaing. I found him in the vehicle compound.

'Everything all right with that truck now?'

'It's fine,' Gaing said. 'Back in the forest tomorrow.'

We were standing under a palm-frond awning and Gaing was filling a can with engine oil from a large drum. 'The engine is good now. Just the oil change. Everything is fine with it.'

'So. Good. Everything's fine then. Good.' What an imbecile I am, I thought. I can't put two words together.

147

Gaing turned to face me, the full can of oil in his hand.

'Any news of Ilpe?' I said.

'He is out of prison now.'

'Will he come back here? To the camp?'

'No. Ilpe will never come back here. It was bad for him here. Maybe he will go back to Philippines. I don't know.'

There was something in the way that Gaing told me all this that made it clear that he would be polite but never friendly. I was fully alone. Cut off. Isolated.

*****

The worst times were the nights. Being busy during the day kept the dreams away. But at night my father's accusing stare haunted me. I had to reply to his letter, but I couldn't bring myself to do it. And more and more the boy's face was re-asserting itself. I had fought him off for so long, but now he was back again. So I worked all day in the forest, and then late into the night in my office. Filing, tidying, doing work that didn't need to be done just then. Anything to tire me. Then I would drink enough to knock me out without giving me too much of a hangover and I would crawl into bed exhausted, spent and hoping that sleep when it came would be dreamless.

The night the lights came on, I thought it must have been a dream. I practically fell out of bed, blinded by the lights streaming in from the vehicle compound. The noises of men running and voices raised added to the sense of confusion. I stumbled across to the door of my room and opened it. Dapo was beating the oildrum and men were running around like chickens with their heads cut off. My first thought was a fire, but there was no smoke, no smell of burning. I put on my trousers, boots and a heavy sweater and went outside.

All the lights in the camp were on. And in the arc lights, the camp looked like a lunar landscape, greyish-brown, large shadows everywhere. The original bedlam seemed to be dying

148

down. Everyone had gotten up, and we were all coming round to working out what was happening.

I saw Arkland standing at the entrance to the vehicle stockade with what looked like a distributor cap in his hand. I went over to Dapo at the cookhouse and told him to stop beating the oildrum. It was very quiet then. No-one moved and there was no noise above the normal forest night noises, the cicadas and the other insects. And that wasn't really noise. That was always there.

'What's happening, Dapo?'

'Penan. Penan man. He came and he no good.' Before I could get any more out of him, Arkland came storming over to us.

'So you got out of your bed at last. Just in time to see your friends' handiwork. Look at what your Penan buddies have done now.'

He thrust the distributor cap into my hands. The plastic head was smashed and the cables were all hacked away.

'Every goddam no-good mother-fucking vehicle immobilised. Every fucking one. And it's all your fault, Mahon, you thick Irish bastard.'

'My fault?'

'Yes, your fault. If you hadn't killed that kid, none of this would have happened. We wouldn't be in this shit. You brought them on us. No vehicles, right? That's your area. Sort it out. And fast.'

Then he turned away from me and almost ran to the office block. He put the light on and I saw him standing in front of his beloved maps.

I walked over to Gaing and he confirmed what Arkland had said. 'All the vehicles. The Cats, the graders, the trucks, the Land Rovers. Every one.'

'All distributor caps?'

'No. Maybe half. Some the starter motors. Some tyres. Different.'

'Who did it?'

'Dapo called me in my bed. Said he was up to pass water.

Saw someone with the vehicles. They ran off when he went over. Maybe a dozen.'

'Penan?'

'Yes.'

'Send the men back to bed.'

'But it's nearly dawn...'

'If what you tell me is true, nobody will be going anywhere today. Send them back to bed.'

I walked through the vehicle compound, checking all the vehicles. We had two graders, for road levelling, four dump trucks, a Land Rover and three caterpillar-tracked bulldozers we used for clearance and dragging logs out of the forest. The large transporters were down at the coast. Lucky for us. If they had been in the vehicle compound we would have had no transport at all. No serious damage had been done. Everything was repairable if we could get the spares. Some we'd have in the stores, most we'd have to bring in. That meant delays. There was something clinical about the way it had been done. There was no mess, no fuss. Just clear and effective sabotage.

'They seemed to know what they were doing,' I said to Gaing when he rejoined me. There was just the two of us now, our multiple shadows overlapping beneath our feet.

He didn't make any reply, but his silence only added to my suspicions.

'Let's get some sleep. We'll look things over more fully in daylight. I don't think we need worry about the Penan coming back tonight, do you?'

'No.'

'No,' I repeated. 'They've got us where they want us now.'

We separated and I went back to my room, convinced that Gaing or someone else had told the forest-dwellers exactly how to bring our fleet to a standstill.

*****

The floor of my room was littered with balls of paper. I had started the letter at least a dozen times and each time I knew I had written too much. I put in everything about the dead boy, about the Penan and our vehicles, about the woman taking my photo, and about being in jail. It was a long, sad outpouring and I crumpled the sheets up and threw them on the floor. I couldn't send him that. So I ended up with a short, terse note which said everything about my father and me.

Dear Dad,

I was delighted to get your letter. And surprised. Thank you for telling me about Gerald. I will write to him. And Mam. I hope she's better now. It must be really hard on her. Tell her I am thinking of her.

I'm very busy here just now. The full monsoon is due any day now and we're probably going to move camp soon. Most of our vehicles are out of commission just now too. Nothing but problems.

Thanks for writing, Dad. It was great to hear from you.

Your loving son,
Lawrence

I tried hard but I couldn't remember a time we'd touched. I knew men didn't do that, especially after a certain age, but I couldn't dredge up from anywhere in my memory one occasion when my father had lain a hand on my shoulder, or touched me on the arm, or patted me on the head. It was the wrong time for me to be going over such old ground. I couldn't understand how it all came together. I sat there in my office, struggling with words for my father, when I should have been in the vehicle stockade overseeing the repair of the vehicles. Or writing reports for Arkland and HQ in Kuala Lumpur. I never had any trouble with composing them. Words came easy to me there. It was just with my father. I couldn't even be warm. I couldn't be human. I had written my letter like a report. It was technical writing without the statistics.

I had spent a long time over single words until I got the final version. I had put in 'prayed' first, but changed that to 'thinking'. My father knew I didn't pray. So did my mother. He would enjoy showing it to her.

Look, Mother, a letter from Larry. Go on, take it. It's Lawrence. He's asking for you. And Gerry. Getting on the best he is. The best.

She would take the single half-covered sheet into her hands and start to cry because she knew that it wasn't really a letter. It was a plea and an accusation. My mother would understand and instead of helping, that only made me feel worse.

*****

'Jesus, Mahon. Are you writing your last will and testament?'

Arkland breezed into my office and kicked at the crumbled balls of paper on the floor. 'You've been in here since morning. What the fuck are you doing?'

He was wearing shorts and a broad-brimmed straw hat of the sort rice farmers on the lowland plains used. His torso was tanned dark brown, making the white fuzz on his chest stand out like thistledown. 'I'm sweating my balls out under the Land Rover and I say, "Let's get Mahon over here. After all, vehicles are his baby. Yeah?"'

He loved a fight. He loved it when the going got tough. He revelled in this role as saviour and Lone Ranger.

'I'm just finishing some paperwork,' I said. 'I left Gaing in charge. I'll join him after lunch. Check how everything is going. We're doing fine.'

'Everything's going fine. Yeah. Just fine. We've lost a full day because we've no vehicles. That, on top of down-time because of the strike. Then our pictures are all over the papers and government heavies are blaming us for distracting the timber minister's daughter. Yeah. Tokyo wants two shiploads by the end of the month. What do they know about it? We've got about one and a half with two weeks to go. Yeah. We're fine, you just catch up on your fucking paperwork.' He kicked a ball of paper and it lifted off and out of the window.

'Yeah. Points on the scoreboard. That's what counts. Yeah. And vehicles on the road. Right, Mahon?'

I said nothing. His back was to me. His upper body was strong. Like a swimmer's. I'd never noticed that before.

'Heh. And put a PS in for your mother. Tell her I said hello.'

Then he limped to the door and slammed it closed after him.

I skipped lunch and went to the vehicle compound. I wanted to check on the mechanics' work before they'd finished their lunch. They'd managed to get most of our fleet up and running. We were back in business.

CHAPTER SIXTEEN

Our vehicles left the compound in convoy the following morning. Last to leave were the graders, moving out to finish access roads at the furthest point from the camp. As they rumbled up the slope and onto the road into the forest, a brand new unmarked Toyota Landcruiser entered the camp. The driver wore a uniform, like a concierge in a fancy hotel in Singapore. The Landcruiser pulled up beside Arkland's office and a man in a tropical suit got out. He looked around for a moment as if getting his bearings then pulled a briefcase out of the vehicle and went up the steps to the office. Almost immediately, Arkland came out and called across the compound to me. I was under the rattan awning taking grease off my hands with industrial cleanser.

'Mahon. Get over here. Now.'

I walked to the office block, past the Landcruiser. The driver hadn't taken his uniform off. All the windows were closed and the large air-conditioning unit on top of the cab was humming. The driver was from the city and he was preserving a little of that special atmosphere no matter where he went.

'This is Jeffrey Embury from the Asia office. And this is Larry Mahon, my assistant. He's the engineer at the camp. Supposed to know what's going on.'

I shook hands with the man in the tropical suit. He was about forty and looked like he would be more comfortable in something dark blue, double-breasted and pinstriped. I planned to say very little. I didn't trust Arkland, and I didn't want to help him save his neck by offering Embury mine.

'We thought it would make sense if we had a chat with you ourselves, Greg, in the first instance,' began Embury. He was taking papers from the briefcase he had rested on his lap. 'Getting the company into the national press outside the usual business and finance pages is always a risky matter. The photographs don't do either of you justice.' He tossed a copy of *The New Straits Times* article onto Arkland's desk.

Arkland wasn't even looking at him. His eyes were fixed on his maps. He might have been planning another assault on it with his coloured pins. But we all knew he was listening. Especially Embury.

'Pak Lee Chung is an important friend to us,' he continued, 'and we can't be seen to aggravate either himself or members of his family. But as you say yourself, Greg, it is very much a local matter and the police have dropped the case. I had a most fruitful discussion with a… Sergeant Merkat earlier this morning.'

By now he had fished out a copy of Arkland's quarterly returns. He turned to the page of projections.

'I see you expect to make all quotas for this month. That still hold?'

Arkland nodded imperceptibly.

'Good. Right. That gives us about two weeks to wind things down. We're suggesting a temporary closure at the end of the month. A suspension of the concession by the Ministry will be announced in the next week. Temporary, of course. You can take a holiday, and in a couple of months time we can start up again. There's sufficient stock-holding of raw logs at our other camps to keep our Japanese customers happy in the short term. Production drops with the monsoon anyway.'

He retrieved his papers, put them back in his briefcase and snapped it shut. 'You're both on full pay, of course. The men can go. Mothball the plant. Treat it like a holiday. Or should I say vacation, Greg. Ha-ha.' It was the first time I'd ever heard a proper toffee-nosed laugh. It was a mixture of the high-pitched tee-hee a spoiled child might make and the raw guffaw of a bully.

Then he got up and reached his hand to Arkland.

'Sorry I can't stay, Greg. As I said, a flying visit. Love to have stayed longer. Gotten a feel for the place. The real thing. We desk-wallahs so rarely get a chance to visit a place like this. But, as I said, must press on.'

Arkland shook his hand without looking at him. Then Embury turned to me.

'I gather there are some difficulties with your family. A brother, I believe. While we're sympathetic, I think you'll appreciate that matters are already sensitive enough here without exacerbating them with unfortunate publicity in the UK connecting a company employee with terrorists. You're already on shaky enough ground here, Mr Mahon.'

Then he left the office and climbed into the Landcruiser. The driver revved it hard and they left the camp with dust blowing behind them. Embury, the first senior official from HQ to visit the camp, had been with us for less than twenty minutes.

'I hope we didn't delay him,' I said, and Arkland laughed a morose chuckle.

'Larry, my boy. That's how the empires are made. First the British Empire. Now Searwood.'

'Who is he?' I asked.

'Jeffrey Embury is General Operations Manager Asia. Translated, as far as we're concerned, that's God. His visitation means that not many people know about this. Only the very big-wigs. They're keeping it sweet for the Minister. And they're dumping it all in my lap. Oh yes!'

'You lied to him about the timber quotas, didn't you?' I said.

'Maybe. Maybe not. We can still make this month's.'

'Not unless we move camp. Or go down into the valley. Either way there will be delays. There just isn't enough timber where we are now.'

'If we don't meet this month's quota, I'm a complete goner. As it is, they're going to try to screw me into the ground on this.'

I left him then. I knew he was right. It would be nothing to Searwood to terminate our contracts and ensure we never worked again. And in my case they could still stick me with killing the boy. Use that as a way of getting out of the contract I had with them.

It was time I started to look out for myself.

*****

156

So many tumbling trees! Great lines of them falling and a boy running through them with a blowpipe in his hand, a parang on his hip, a laughing boy with my brother's face and hair, but brown Penan skin and the speed of a forest deer, running through the tumbling trees towards my Land Rover. My hands were locked on the steering wheel, my feet were frozen on the pedals. The boy ran towards me. And the trees crashed round me.

I woke up as the boy jumped onto the Land Rover bonnet and pressed his face against the windscreen. My brother's face behind the glass. That final image was reflected finally in the basin of water I doused my face in, trying to come round. It was still dark. And intensely cold. I put on some clothes and sat in a chair, drying my face with a towel. It was my first nightmare in weeks.

'I'm an engineer,' I said to myself. 'I deal in realities. Hard facts. If I could just get them together on paper in front of me everything will be all right.' I pulled the chair up to my desk and got a sheet of paper and a pen. 'Make a list. Then plan.'

But the page stayed blank. My arm couldn't move the pen. It was worse than trying to write a letter home. I finally got up and went to the cookhouse to look for some coffee. It would be dawn soon. I tried to convince myself that an early start to the day would be the best thing for me.

The compound was quiet. The forest was quiet, the short hush before the awesome dawn chorus. There were no stars. There would be early-morning rain, a monsoon sign. We'd never make the month's quota now, especially when the rains really came.

There was a light in the cookhouse. Two men were sitting with a pot of coffee at a table with two candles. I recognised Gaing as he stood up. The other man was Ilpe.

'You are early,' said Gaing.

'I couldn't sleep,' I said.

Ilpe spoke rapidly in Malay, and Gaing replied sharply, putting his hand on Ilpe's shoulder as he began to get out of his seat.

'Ilpe is here to get some things. He is going back to the Philippines.'

'That's good.' I still hadn't moved from the doorway of the cookhouse. For the first time ever since I'd begun my life overseas, I really felt like I didn't belong.

Ilpe said something and Gaing silenced him before asking me, 'You want some coffee?'

'Well, yes. Coffee then.'

I moved over towards their table. Their shadows were huge behind them. As I came nearer, Ilpe pushed his chair back roughly, stood up and walked away. Gaing called something out to him. I poured myself a cup of coffee. It smelt fresh and felt hot in the metal cup.

'You're going back to the Philippines, Ilpe? Have you got a job there?' I asked.

'He will stay with his sister for a while. Then he will find work. There will be a lot of work for drivers,' Gaing answered for him.

'Of course. Especially with Ilpe's experience.'

Ilpe was in deep shadow, too far away from the table for the candles to light up any part of him. Suddenly he loomed back into view, leaning across the table, glaring at me.

'You and Mr Arkland. You are my experience. After this place I can learn nothing. I will never forget you, Mahon. Or Mr Arkland. Especially Mr Arkland.' Then he was gone, back into the shadows, and his darkened shape moved out of the cookhouse, his shoes scuffling on the wooden floorboards.

'Why did he come back here?' I asked.

'For some things. I told you. He's very angry.'

'Is he dangerous?'

'We are all dangerous, Mr Mahon,' Gaing replied. 'You, me. Mr Arkland. This forest is a dangerous place.'

I looked at Gaing in the candlelight. I regretted I had not made more of our friendship at the start. Now he looked at me with a deep mistrust. Almost hate. I knew he was too decent a man really to feel hate. But he was close to it.

'Do you know the concession will probably have to close?' I shouldn't have spoken to him about that, but I was trying to soften the look in his eyes. In the bleakness of the pre-dawn light, I was searching for some fellowship. 'I mean, if these troubles continue. The barricades, the breakdowns.'

'And the men?'

'I don't know. It's up to Arkland.'

He knew exactly what would happen if the concession closed. I was hedging my bets, tipping the scales in my favour. As Arkland might have said, I was looking after Number One.

I finished my coffee. 'Must be nearly dawn now. I might as well take a bucket bath and pretend I'm really awake.'

I got up and walked to the door. The area in front of me was taking on that light-brown colour it always had just before dawn. The forest sounds were rising. Some men moved towards their communal bathing and toilet area.

'Why did Ilpe come back?' I asked over my shoulder.

'To kill Arkland. Maybe to kill you. But it's okay. I have spoken to him.'

I walked across to my room and took off my clothes. In the yard behind my room I filled bucket after bucket of water from the metal drum used for my bath. My teeth chattered as the cold water poured over me and my skin turned blue. I kept filling the buckets and pouring on the water. I was punishing myself. Or preparing myself, like a swimmer training to cross the Channel.

*****

Would I be sorry to leave this place? I wondered as I climbed out of the cab of a grader I had been driving all day. It was nearly five in the evening. The sun was lowering in the sky, down by the sea. Up here in the mountains the heat of the day rose from the forest around me. I was on the stretch of road where the boy had been killed. The grader was parked almost exactly on the spot where the Land Rover had run him over. I felt bitter pangs of guilt and regret about his death, but these had been deadened by the time that had passed.

As sometimes happens in the rainforest, there is a lull in the constant noise of bird and animal life. Such a lull happened as I stood beside the grader, and in that silence came the thought that I really would miss this place when the concession closed. There would be other forests for me to work in. At least in the short term. But somehow this place had been special, had a special effect on me. With the boy's death had come new knowledge. I would never work in places like this in the same way again. The boy changed everything.

I clambered back into the driver's seat. We were short of drivers without Ilpe. We hadn't felt it really up to now, with the strike and everything. Now I had every man I could get out in the forest clearing the last of the logs from the upland area in order to meet the monthly target due before the concession was formally closed. I figured doing that was important for my long-term job prospects with Searwood. Or with anyone else. Embury had warned me. I wanted the process of closing down the concession to go well. I didn't want to give the company any more excuses than they already had for getting rid of me. I was bringing all the graders back in after tidying up some stretches of road. I was going to mothball all the plant. I was going to do a first-class job of covering myself.

I turned the grader in a wide arc. The big orange-red sun, low in the sky, shone straight into the cab as I drove back to the camp. It gave everything a dull gold colour, like this was the most blessed place on earth and I was doing the work of the gods. Only in the rainforests have I ever felt like that.

CHAPTER SEVENTEEN

When I got back, I went to Arkland's office to see if he'd brought me any mail from his visit to the town. He wasn't there, but on his desk there was a pile of letters from head office, as well as some newspapers. I picked up a *New Straits Times*. It was days old. The headline story was of an ASEAN conference in Bangkok. I turned the page and my picture stared out at me again. This time I was paired with Ilpe, under a headline: 'Government Bows to Pressure on Forest Murder Cover-Up'.

In the article there was speculation that the concession was about to be closed and that a full inquiry was to be launched into the death of the Penan boy:

> Two people, Lawrence Mahon, an engineer at the concession, and Ilpe Tongishu, a Filipino driver, have been interviewed about the case by the police in Borneo. No charges have been brought though police enquiries are continuing.

Arkland's uneven footfalls sounded behind me.

'See that! You're getting all the fame. The media just love you, Larry boy. I'm right outa the picture now.' He came round behind me and threw himself into a chair. 'Jesus. The heat! The sooner this monsoon comes the better.'

'We'll probably be closed anyway. It won't matter to us.'

'You don't say.'

I'd never liked that playful tone in his voice. I prodded the newspaper with my finger. 'The newspapers know we're going to close. Somebody must have leaked the story in Kuala Lumpur. We'll be getting the official notice any day now.'

'We won't be getting anything like that, Larry me boy. No sir. We've had it from Searwood. Old Embury told us what to do. They've put a flyer in the newspaper. But damn sure they're not going to make any of this official. Nothing on paper to us. What you're holding in your hand is the nearest we're going to get to an official order to close the concession. That newspaper story. And this telegram.' He tossed a small brown envelope at me. I used the newspaper to catch it.

I opened the envelope and read the four words in the middle of the telegram sheet:

ADVISE ON PROGRESS STOP.

They meant nothing to me so I said that to Arkland.

'Then we must enlighten you, my friend. In the top left-hand corner you will see the coding Searwood SEA, which is the only clue that Embury may have written this telegram. But I know it's from him as sure as I've known him for seven years and this company nearly ten. You see, he wants me to reply that I've closed the concession, just like he laid out when he visited. Or at least give him a date when I plan to close it. He wants me to tell him that I've let all the men go, that I've mothballed the plant and that I've headed off to Hawaii for some much needed R and R.'

'So?'

'So? Larry me boy, your naiveté should be attractive in one so young, but not in this fucking place it's not!' He slammed his fist onto his desk making the papers shimmy about. Then he began pacing up and down behind his desk, the slow kalumpf of his wounded leg marking time as he spoke. 'They want me to close the concession. Nothing official. They want it to be all my idea, so that it can be all my fault. If things go well and the heat dies down, they can quietly restart, claim there was a temporary hitch and bring in a new guy to run the concession. If the mega-shit hits the fan they can blame me, label me a loony and a no-gooder. And damage limitation is what Embury is really best at. They'll be back here under a new name and with a new boy in charge inside a year. You get it now or are you a complete dumbo?' The veins in his temples stood out as he roared the last words at me.

I should have hit him then. I could have. I was angry enough. I was panicked enough. And he deserved it. Things might have worked out better if I had hit him. But fear was stronger than anger so I just put the telegram back on his desk, folded the newspaper and put it back too. There was another telegram envelope I hadn't noticed before on the desk. It was addressed to me and I picked it up.

'You got it now, Mahon? That clear enough for you? They're trying to screw Arkland good and proper. And you know something? They're going to get one fuck of a surprise when I reply to that telegram. I'm going to say: "Progress excellent. Commencing logging Sector Three, the valley sector, immediately. Quotas to be exceeded." Yessiree, we're going down into the valley. I want you to get that road in pronto. They want to close this concession, they're going to have to come here and do it themselves. Nobody, and I mean nobody, is going to fuck with Arkland. You listening to me, Mahon?'

I don't know if I was listening to him or not. I knew I couldn't hear him. There was an awful ratcheting in my ears. I felt a lightness in my bowels like they were going to empty. I reread my telegram, scrunched it into a ball and stuffed it into my pocket. Arkland was screaming at me as I turned and walked out of his office into the steamy night.

*****

When I was a boy the arrival of a telegram meant only one thing. Trouble. The worst trouble you could get. Death. Telegrams meant death. Then a period of shock and bags packed for the journey to a distant wake and funeral. What confused me first about my telegram was that the name of the sender was given as Mick Gallagher. I couldn't initially understand why Mick Gallagher would be sending me a telegram but then it was all so clear:

GERALD DECEASED STOP CONTACT HOME IMMEDIATELY STOP CONDOLENCES STOP MICK GALLAGHER.

Who else but Mick Gallagher could send a telegram on my brother's death? Mother? No, she would be too stricken. My father? Anger would blind him. There was no other close family. Uncles in West Donegal and Scotland on my father's side. A spinster aunt, my mother's sister, sightless and maintained by neighbours in a cottage near Fintona. No, nothing could be done by my family. Only Mick Gallagher could do it. Only he would have the nerve in the face of a violent death. And I knew even as I read the telegram that Gerald must have died violently. He was in prison, wasn't he? He was a young man wasn't he? He's hung himself, I thought. He's been beaten by warders. He's cut his throat. He's jumped out of a moving van. I had all these pictures in my head. But they were all replaced by one glaring memory of my brother Gerald. He was about six. I was about fifteen. I don't know exactly. But I had been taking him to the swimming baths on a regular basis for weeks in high summer. My friends jeered at me for wanting to play with weans. I just said, 'He's my brother and he wants to learn to swim.'

Then one day, when the great windows that ran the length of the swimming pool were filled with a sky of tropical blue, Gerald took off. He slipped like an eel out of my hands and I just managed to stifle the impulse to scream and grab him as he squirmed away from me. His black trunks and his black head were the two visible humps of the monster he made as he churned across the pool. Then he grabbed the side and surfaced. Water running off his face couldn't hide the smile in his eyes and on his lips as he gasped for breath.

'You did it, Gerald, you did it,' I shouted as he gagged and gagged, and finally smiled a smile brighter than the sunlight filling the water and the air.

*****

I turned to Arkland in desperation. I was alone. Confused. He was the only other white man in the place. I could have been Gaing's friend, but I had let him down. I had let them all down. The men. My family. My brother. I hadn't taken care of him like an older brother should. I felt worthless and brutish. I reckoned me and Arkland were the same all right. Epiphytes, rotting on the branch of some great tree.

'My brother's dead. At home they would be waking him now. Let's have a bit of a wake for my brother,' I said as I walked into Arkland's room.

He was working at a desk and had a look of surprise on his face. 'Your brother's dead? That telegram today?'

I nodded, and poured two large measures of whiskey from the bottle I had brought. 'Black Bush. Only the best. I've been saving it and this seems like a good time.'

'You want to go home?' asked Arkland as he took the glass. I had been asking myself that question ever since I read the telegram. It hadn't really surprised me to realise that I didn't want to go home.

'No. I don't think so. What's the point? He's dead, isn't he?'

The whiskey didn't taste as strong as I usually found it. I drank it down, glass after glass, until Arkland's room began to spin around me and I collapsed on the floor. Arkland's damaged left leg loomed beside me as I dragged myself up again.

'Get along to bed, Larry me boy. We'll need you fighting fit if we're going to show those bastards back at Headquarters. And we are, you know, Larry. We're just going to run this little old concession right and sweet.'

I staggered along the walkway to my room and fell into bed. I was lucid enough to know I'd have an awful head the following morning. But I also hoped that I would sleep and that there would be no dreams. I almost smiled lying there, thinking of my dead brother and watching the ceiling revolve above me.

*****

I tossed and turned but could not sleep. Confused pictures of my family raced round my head until I reached for the photo I had brought back with me. It showed the four of us in the stunned poses easily recognisable as a self-timed photo. God, how it pained me to remember Gerald dashing around, calling out instructions.

Keep saying cheese, folks. Only one more to go.
Setting the camera on a pile of books on the table.
They'll fall off. Will you look what you're doing?
My father had to say something.
Just keep saying cheese. Won't be a minute.
Gerald holding us all together.
Your father doesn't even like cheese, Gerald.

My mother's matter-of-factness made us all burst out laughing. Finally, the camera was judged to be balanced and propped at the right height and angle and Gerald set the timer. A tiny red flashing light showed it was counting down to the flash. Then off it went and that was it.

Now I held the results in my hand. All those manoeuvres. All that laughter. All those tiny relationships, attitudes and emotions that make up a family focused into this sliver of paper with the painted images of us facing out. Even as I stared at it through my tears, Gerald's impish face turned up to me seemed to be fading. Going away from me. That was how it was. A tiny flashing red light showed the counter was on. It started at birth. I was already a boy when Gerald came, and now the flash had come for him and I was still here. It seemed wrong. I should have been first.

I tried to make sense of how they must be feeling at home. My mother would be shattered, I knew that for certain. My father trying hard to see off the confusion he must be feeling. Standing there always holding a newspaper, as if in concentrating on the world at large he could hold at bay the tragedy that had befallen them. Would it be a paramilitary funeral? I wondered. It terrified me to realise that I didn't even know the answer to that. I sat up in the bed still staring at the photograph.

What was I really part of? What had I to hold onto that was real in my life? I had my work, yes. I had the whole world of the rainforests to placate and tame, to negotiate and calm. Travel in exotic places. The challenge of being overseas. But what did it all amount to? I had to go and see. So I climbed out of bed, lucid in the way that drunks sometimes are, and staggered out of my room, still holding the photo.

I stood outside on the boardwalk and looked at the compound. This is what I had. The monochrome light making boxed shadows of the buildings that surrounded the compound. The careless limitless toss of stars that arched above me. The moon eyeing me coldly. But always the darkness and the void beyond the light. This is what I had in the face of Gerald's death. The screech of the cicadas drowned my sobs and I stumbled off the boardwalk. There had to be more.

A wedge of light came from Arkland's office. I moved towards it and, stepping onto the boardwalk, I could see into the room where he sat at his desk. I moved into the shadows to avoid being seen, though I had no idea why I should be spying on him. He sat poring over papers, but he didn't seem to be working. His eyes were sunken holes hollowed deep into his head as he stared at his desk. Once he looked up, and the awful emptiness of those eyes made me flinch. His maps behind him dotted with coloured pins. A single bulb casting a remorseless light around him. He is so lonely, I thought to myself. He has no-one. Not even me. And as if to prove this Arkland seemed to lurch forward and put his face in his hands, bending low over the desk. He told me he never slept. Now I knew why. He had no-one. He had nothing worth dreaming about. There had to be more in it for me.

I turned and looked around me. In the distance the Macks and Cats loomed like prehistoric beasts in the vehicle stockade. The squat forms of the bunkhouses drew me. There would be something there for me. I staggered across the compound, marvelling at the crisp shadows the moonlight made under me, swirling and moving from back to front, until I climbed the steps of the first bunkhouse. I pushed open a door gently. A low-wattage bulb shone grimly, as if these loggers and timber workers were afraid of the dark. When my eyes adjusted, I was able to make out the men asleep in the bunks. Hulking shapes felled by sleep. Groans and snores and little whimpers. Were these the demons that challenged the great trees with their saws and their trucks? Sleeping there, without their hard hats and the whine of their saws, they were lost children.

'Mahon. What is the problem?'

It was Gaing. I could just make out his head from the nearest bunk. I put my finger to my lips and made a soundless whistle. He moved as if he was going to get up. But I signalled to him not to and he settled again, looking questioningly at me. I backed out of the bunkhouse, closing the door and sighing to myself as I rested against the rough wood of the building. I knew I couldn't tell Gaing about Gerald. We weren't friends enough for that. I looked at the photo and gulped on the sobs in my throat. How did I come to be so alone? I even lost the only brother I had, and I never really knew him.

My anguish drove me across the compound again, this time towards the vehicle stockade. It was a world I knew. A world in which I felt comfortable. These mechanical beasts offered me certainty and solace. I knew all about their ageing and death. A clapped-out machine was something I could manage. Even the violent death of a machine in a rockslide did nothing to scare me. I knew their cycles of life and death. Their rites of passage. I leaned against the curving blade of a Cat, clods of earth stuck to it here and there. The solid coolness of the metal supported me and I looked up at the sky. Such a vastness. So much of it all. I felt puny and lost, trying to hide in the embrace of the earthmover. Tears ran down my cheeks, and I whimpered and muttered to myself the terrifying questions facing all humans in the face of death.

What does it mean? How will I cope?

I stepped round the blade and climbed into the cab, into the very womb of the vehicle. I held the photo in front of me and sobbed in great heaves for my dead brother and for myself, feeling lost and alone. If any of the men had risen then they would have found one of their bosses sitting in the cab of a vehicle, crying and calling softly for his mother as the moon looked coldly on and the stars straddled the void, oblivious to it all.

CHAPTER EIGHTEEN

The next day, my tongue stuck to the roof of my mouth, I met Arkland in the cookhouse. Dapo poured me a cup of coffee as I sat down beside Arkland. 'How d'you feel?' he asked.

'Okay,' I lied.

'Right. Good. I want you down in the valley sector today. Get it surveyed fast. And then get the heavy stuff down there. I want us felling later this week, clearing those shadows, getting some light on the ground, so let's get a road in there.' He got up and left, and I kept swirling the coffee round in my mug. I was sure I would just vomit if I drank it.

Then, instead of sending a telegram home saying that I would be there for the funeral, I put my surveying gear into the rear of the Land Rover. Instead of getting to the railhead as fast as I could, I drove out of the camp, taking the road north into the forest and then turning down the stretch of road I had put in when preliminary surveys of the valley sector were being made. Instead of going home for my brother's funeral, I went down into the valley and began to prepare to open it up for logging.

I wanted to hide in the forest. I wanted the forest to save me. I couldn't face the news from home, so I buried myself in my work. I hid in the forest. Something about the quiet in the rainforest has always calmed me. The birds and the animals, the shushing of the leaves and the irregular distant thump as a great tree falls; it's as if none of these noises is intrusive. None of them is noise. It isn't until the buzz of the chainsaw, the rumble of the caterpillar track, the crunching gear changes of the Land Rover come along that you really hear anything to disturb you.

As I surveyed in the valley floor that morning, only the slurp of my boots through the muddy undergrowth disturbed the silence. The silence of the great forest. The trees keeping their secrets even as I planned their felling. The silence of the grave.

When I look back on this time, I know I didn't consciously make a decision to stay at the camp. It amazes me to realise that if I had rushed home for my brother's funeral, I would have been saved from the horrors and humiliations that came later. Why didn't I go home? I could have used Gerald's death as a way out of the crisis building around Arkland. But I didn't. My main emotion at the time, and I recall this clearly, was a sort of shock. A great lethargy. I was on automatic pilot. I was switched off. I was hiding in my work in the forest, as I had done so often before. I wasn't facing up to anything. And yet I was also wilfully agreeing to stay at the concession. The sense that a crisis was coming to a head also convinced me that I couldn't leave. Not just then.

'People die at such inconvenient times.' That phrase actually came into my head, and I couldn't help but think about the young Penan boy. And about my brother.

*****

In the end, I arranged that Arkland would send a telegram home:
CAN'T COME HOME STOP SORRY STOP LAWRENCE.
I had to, otherwise my family or Mick Gallagher would try to contact me via the company. Maybe they were already doing that.

I knew my family would put a brave face on it. And the funeral would go ahead.

'I sent your telegram. You might want to change your mind when you see this.'

Arkland threw me a copy of *The New Straits Times* as he climbed onto the boardwalk in front of the offices. It was almost dark and great sheets of rain marched across the compound, from the cookhouse to the office block. Everything was grey and muffled, as if Noah's floods had returned. 'It started just as I left the village. I hope this fucker isn't the monsoon. I hope it's just our daily dose. But I don't know. Smells like monsoon. Sort of putrid stuff coming from deep in that valley. When are we going to get loggers down there, Mahon?'

I pretended I didn't hear him. I wanted to read the news item again. Ten lines in a narrow column. My brother's death notice in the 'International News Round' column of *The New Straits Times*:

Prisoners Killed in Escape Bid

Belfast. Two IRA men were shot dead by soldiers in a foiled escape bid from the Crown Court in Belfast. They were Gerald Mahon and Michael Curran, both from Londonderry. They were before Justice Hamilton on charges of IRA membership and attempted murder when they made their escape bid using handguns smuggled into the court. Armed soldiers opened fire as the pair ran across an outside yard to a waiting car. The car, driven by a man wearing a black hood, drove away in the direction of West Belfast. Police are asking for witnesses.

My own brother carrying a handgun. My own brother shot. I couldn't believe it. And yet there it was, in print.

'Your brother seems to have been a bit of a wild one. Bit of a Billy the Kid character, was he?'

How could I answer Arkland's question? I hardly knew my brother. When I tried to get a picture of him in my mind, I kept seeing a boy, a young boy with the face of a mature man. And he was swimming. Or running behind me on our way home from school. I couldn't see him with a gun. Not Gerald.

'I didn't really know him. He was a lot younger than me.'

'I never had no brothers and sisters. Always a loner.'

I looked across at Arkland and he caught my eye. He was about to say something, something that would have linked us and made sense of our being there. But he thought better of it, turned round to face his maps and said, 'We've got to get loggers down there, Mahon. We've got to concentrate. If you're with me, we can do it. Sometimes that's the only way to face it. Together. Stonewalling it. Nam. The Philippines. Here.'

It was the nearest I'd heard him come to expressing emotion. I could see his back and the pins stuck in the maps. Words almost came to my lips. Words about my brother, the dead Penan boy, lost opportunities, such a jumble of words that they blocked each other. I said nothing, took the newspaper and walked out of the office, leaving Arkland facing his maps.

*****

I sent the loggers down into the valley the next day. Mack dumpers, each with ten loggers in the back. Our full squad. I sent the Cats after them. The yard reverberated with the sound of vehicles revving up. The men were all excited. New prospects, more work. The uncertainty of all the past weeks behind us. Dapo stood on the step of the kitchen block. He was jiggling from one foot to the other. He waved as the trucks moved out. Arkland was at his desk as I called in through the window slats.

'There they go.'

'Good. Good. You get down there too. Keep them at it. We need those logs.'

He said this without raising his head from his papers. Same old Arkland. Harsh and direct. But I felt a lift in my step as I moved along to my own office. We were back in business and work would solve everything. Or at least it would help keep everything at bay.

I worked at my desk for the morning. I loved the quiet undisturbed hours, raising my head every now and then to see the shadows move across the compound. Dapo came to the door of the kitchen and tossed a plate of leftovers at the clutch of scrawny chickens that he kept with wilful disregard for their health. Otherwise the camp was quiet. I didn't see Arkland until I went across to the kitchen to get something to eat. He was sitting alone with a heaped plate of fried rice and a mug of coffee in front of him. I nodded at Dapo and wagged a finger, enough to tell him I wanted the same.

'You're still here!' Arkland said belligerently.

'I'll go after I get something to eat. I got the paperwork up to

172

date. A survey report, some final figures for the projections, a few other bits and pieces. I'll leave them on your desk before I go.'

Dapo brought me a plate of fried rice. I began to wolf it down.

'I met Ilpe a few nights ago.'

'Where?' said Arkland, without ceasing to spoon the fried rice into his mouth.

'Here. Middle of the night. He was talking to Gaing.'

'Ilpe.' Arkland shook his head and made a clucking sound with his tongue. Then he pulled a piece of bush pig from his mouth and using his teeth and his fingers, he tried to rip it apart. 'What did he want?'

'I'm not sure really. Gaing said something silly about Ilpe wanting to kill us. You especially.'

Arkland kept pulling at the piece of meat in his teeth. He separated some gristle and put it on the table beside his plate.

'Ilpe wants to kill me? Whatever for?'

The laugh never really left Arkland's voice. Sometimes you couldn't hear it properly but it never fully disappeared. It was coming through loud and clear now.

'What an ungrateful thing to want to do. But you know something, Mahon? I'm not surprised to have my charity thrown back in my face.'

'What do you mean?'

'Let me tell you about Ilpe. He comes from a stinking hole in Olangapo, on Subic Bay, where the only thing you can get for certain is the pox. Well, I knew his sister; another ungrateful bitch that couldn't wash a man's shirt and who dragged every last aunt, uncle, cousin, niece or nephew out of the sticks to sponge off me. Ilpe was one of them. I'd come home and he'd be eating my dinner. Can you believe that? Then he cleared off to Manila on money his sister stole from me. I kicked her out then. She wasn't even a good lay. Years later Ilpe turned up in Sandakan and I got sentimental and gave him a job. Then I gave him one here. Another mistake. You did me a favour, Larry, killing that kid. You got rid of Ilpe for me. And I don't think he'll be back again.'

I stopped spooning the fried rice into my mouth and pushed my plate away from me. Arkland continued eating, sometimes using his hands, sometimes using his spoon. I stared at him, tried to make some pattern out of the lines on his face, and trying to quell the loathing I felt for him. Why had I fastened myself to him? What force bound me to him so that I couldn't go home for my brother's funeral? Instead I would stay here and do Arkland's bidding despite the disasters I knew must come.

'I'll get down into the valley.' I stood and took two long draughts of coffee, feeling the gritty dregs swirl in the cavities in my teeth.

*****

The seat and the steering wheel of the Land Rover were red hot to the touch when I sat in. No-one and nothing stirred in the midday heat. I could see smoke curling up behind the kitchen block, where Arkland was finishing his lunch and Dapo was boiling rice for the men's return. I drove up the logging road and looked at the green-covered hills in the distance. They weren't part of this concession, but would probably be part of the next one.

I had to pull over to let two logging trucks pass me. The drivers waved as they went by. Each truck carried about ten logs measuring a metre across. The engineer in me made a quick volume calculation. Estimating the length at about five metres gave us maybe forty cubic metres of timber per truck. Loads like that alone wouldn't make the quota for this month. We had to get logs out of the valley sector. Still, we had plenty of men down there. There was still some time.

When the road forked, I headed down towards the valley floor. As I got nearer the work area I realised that I hadn't seen any Cats pulling out logs. I would have expected that by now. Then I saw the two dump trucks side by side in the clearing at the end of the road. Groups of loggers were gathered around two low fires. I smelled coffee being boiled as I climbed out of the Land Rover.

'What's happening?' I said to Gaing when he came towards me. He had driven one of the dumpers. He gestured for me to follow him and we went round to the front of the dumper trucks. Ahead of us, about fifty metres away, the Penan stood. There were about fifty of them, mostly men. They all seemed to be carrying blowpipes. At the front was the old headman who had come to the camp. Beside him was the photographer.

'They were here when we came. They say no logging. This is a sacred place to them.'

'You spoke to them?'

'Yes.'

'Are they dangerous?'

Gaing looked at me and shrugged. I shouldn't have asked.

'Let's get down there and talk to them again.' He appeared to hesitate about following me, but then he did. Loyalty of some sort, I suppose. As we approached the Penan the photographer put the camera to her eyes, swivelled the lens and took our photographs. The headman came forward and four young men followed him, forming up behind him in a row.

'Ask him what must we do.'

Gaing spoke in Penan and the headman answered him. I watched his lips and arms move as he made a long speech. He was a small man, lean and lithe. Heavy rings hung from his earlobes and dangled in loops along his jaw. He wore a rattan pillbox hat with feathers, and had a parang in his loincloth. Gaing translated for me:

'I am Along Lat. I am with my people, Penan people. This is our ancient forest. Our ancestors are here around us. We have our life here. And then the Company comes with the trucks and the chainsaws. Soon there will be no forest. Soon there will be no squirrel, no deer, no fish, no monkey. No Penan. Jaam Sega had a boy who is now dead. You know this, white man. So now, Penan say no more. You will take no logs from here. Along Lat says go now. Penan want no more deaths.'

I knew that I would remember this man and his dignity long after I left the forest. I told Gaing to thank him and to say

I would radio the camp. I walked back to the Land Rover and raised Arkland on the radio.

'We've got a Penan blockade here. A big one. They mean to stop us. Over.'

'Don't fuck me about, Mahon. You're either in this or you're not. Get logs down this road fast. You hear me? Over.'

'I hear you. Over.'

'So.' Arkland's voice had calmed to the edgy cajolery he used when he was threatening me. 'Like I said, Larry boy, we've got to stick together. So you get the loggers in there. I'll call Merkat and get the cops up there. Tell the fuck-shit Penan that. Then get some logs down here. I'm going down to the jetty to get the shipment together. Let's not fuck this one up, eh, Mahon? Over and out.'

The radio went dead. I mouthed 'Or else' to myself. Then I looked at the Penan group. The headman, Along Lat, was still to the front, his guard behind him. Gaing stood slightly to the left of him. And between them I could see the photographer, the telephoto lens cradled in one arm as she gestured to Gaing with the other. I had seen a madwoman wave like that in Melaka. She was in the middle of a road slicked with rain. Cars and buses tried to get around her as she pirouetted slowly in the middle of the road. Men hung out of cars and whistled at her nakedness. I saw her arm wave above her head, like a ballerina. I turned my gaze away. The madwoman made me think of my mother. And now the photographer waved in the same way, without the pirouetting, stirring the air above her head. Not crazy. Strong. I walked back to the Penan until I stood next to Gaing.

'Tell them the police are coming. They must let us in now.'

Gaing told them in Penan and then said, 'That's a bad idea.'

'It's Arkland's idea.'

'You can't hide behind Arkland all the time.' He was almost friendly. And I knew he was right.

The Penan headman went back to the main group. After he had spoken to them, women came forward with children. Then in family groups they came forward and formed a solid line across the road.

Along Lat spoke to the photographer and she shouted in English: 'The Penan will stay here. This is their place. Bring the police. Bring the army. This is their forest. They will stay here.'

'Your father will not protect you if the police come,' I shouted back. I saw her flinch as I said that.

Then she shouted back: 'My father is not my father any more. He is destroying the forest. He is killing the Penan. Just like you, *orang puteh*. The blood of Jaam Sega's boy is on your hands. And if other blood is spilled it will also be on your hands.'

The boy's face in the windscreen came to me again. Knowing his father's name made it worse. Then I imagined the scene when the police came. What if they opened fire? It had happened on another concession. I couldn't face another death. I turned to Gaing.

'I'm going back. I'm going to get Arkland to call the police off. Gather up the men and bring them back to the camp.'

I turned away quickly and walked to the Land Rover. I tried to raise Arkland on the radio but reckoned he had already left for the jetty. My shins itched like crazy and I scratched them until the weals bled.

I drove away as the men clambered into the backs of the dump trucks. I'd had enough. I was going to call off the police.

And then I would tell Arkland I was finished.

*****

Arkland wasn't there when I got to the camp. I went straight to his office and tried to raise Merkat at the police station.

'This is Camp K4 at Long Samedu Concession. Calling Sergeant Merkat. Over.'

'Merkat here. Over.'

'Mahon here. Arkland has called for police up here. I want to call them off. Everything is okay. We don't need them. Over.'

'Ah, Mr Mahon. You are having a busy time up there. Now you don't want us to come? Over.'

'That's right. Everything is under control. Over.'

'Ah, yes! We will stand down, Mr Mahon. Call us anytime. We are only too pleased to be of assistance. Over and out.'

I got off the radio and wrote a short note of resignation and left it on Arkland's desk. Then I headed for the Land Rover. I was going to leave. I was going to pack it all in, but I couldn't do that without finishing with Arkland.

CHAPTER NINETEEN

Seeing the ocean as I drove down to the coast always gave my spirits a lift. And that afternoon the glistening crescent nestling on the horizon convinced me that I had to get out. That I was making the right decision and that I could carry it out.

I swung down through the lower reaches of the forest, regenerating as scrub where we had logged, and soon gained the river, the Sungei Merah, a tributary of the Padas. Here it was slow and sluggish, so different from the streams upland that formed it. Like a knife cutting through fine fabric, a long canoe glided along the middle of the river. The lone oarsman sat at the prow, gently urging his craft along with slow, sweeping strokes, first to starboard then to port with his short single oar. He was wearing a canvas hat, perhaps a remnant of some military campaign, left behind by a soldier who had come to take part in a colonial or international spat. And all that remained in local life was the hat, worn by the fisherman atop his lean brown body, naked except for the shorts just visible above the edge of the canoe.

I pulled into the side of the road and braked, leaving the engine running. I watched the river below me, a wide curve linking the boundless stretches of forest. There were dogs sitting in the rear of the canoe. Brown mongrels, lithe and alert, they sat facing the banks, their ears avidly forward, their back legs primed for the leap. Between them and the man lay rattan fishing traps, big baskets, wide at one end and narrow at the other. I could see nets and the shaft of a blowpipe. Then I saw a roll of matting. Maybe he was delivering it further up river. I knew there were Dayak villages along the lower reaches. I had visited some of them and sat on mats like that in longhouses with the low light of oil lamps and the soft murmurings of communal living.

The man made a series of neat clipping strokes and turned his canoe, following the bend of the river. The dogs adjusted their positions, sniffing at each other in shared excitement. The wake of the canoe fanned out behind the boat in a wonderful chevron that shattered into gently clashing ripples as it reached the two banks. I watched the man's back and the dogs' alert stances until the bend of the river hid them from me and only the fading chevron reminded me of their passage.

All of a sudden the answer to a puzzle that had been bugging me for weeks came to me. I had wondered about the photographer. Why would she do it? Why would she leave the comfort of the city and the pleasure of a rich home to live in the forest? Seeing the man in the canoe gave me my first insight. The dense forest. The quiet river. The small groups of people who made this place their home. Something about all of that brought her to this place.

I could now see how we were linked. We were both outsiders and as such we were joined in a ritualised dance in the forest. My part was the dark. Her's was the light. We swirled around each other, she wearing a dress as blue as the sky, me in a cloak of red. In her hand she carried her camera. In mine a chainsaw snarled. We moved and pirouetted under the great vaulting trees, shafts of light crossing the dark space between us. We were like shadows to each other. It was as if the forest existed only for us. Around us the people of the forest stood in groups, just at the edge of the glade where our dance carried on, until the photographer spun close to me and I saw her twirl away to join the people in the forest. There she stood holding hands with the boy.

I was all alone, standing in the centre of the dance-floor, my red cloak dripping blood, my chainsaw heavy with the flesh of the great trees.

The loud clatter of the Land Rover engine beginning to overheat brought me out of my reverie and I looked down on a river now completely calm as if nothing had passed on it since time began. I took my face in my hands, covering my eyes and mouth. I screamed into my palms, trying to rid my head of all demons. Then I crunched the engine into gear and drove out of the forest.

*****

When I reached the coast, I turned left, away from the town where Merkat and his men had just stood down. Instead, I headed for the river mouth and the jetty we had built. There was a stretch of beach edged with casuarina trees in clumps. Here and there on the sands were giant logs, mainly meranti, that had escaped from the rafts we floated out to the ships. There was a ship at anchor out in the bay. A tug was drawing a raft of logs, maybe a hundred of them, ready for loading for shipment onward to Japan to become scaffolding or disposable chopsticks.

I drove along the track behind the beach and bumped over the wooden bridge that was in constant need of repair because of the heavy loads of logs crossing on the Macks. A loader, its forks high like some prehistoric dinosaur, was parked in front of the cabin that served as bunkhouse and office. I guessed the men were taking a break while the tug delivered the raft of logs to the ship. I looked around for Arkland on the jetty. I first thought that he wasn't there. Then I saw his head above the edge of the jetty. I knew he was standing on a raft of logs in the river. He was pulling a heavy steel cable, trying to get it round one of the steel uprights jutting above him.

'What the fuck are you doing here?' Arkland shouted when he saw me. 'Get over here fast. Grab this.'

I reached down and took the loop on the cable from him and we got it round the upright. Arkland moved further out on the raft, as the logs below him moved in the water. There were about fifty of them, steel cables looping them together and secured by the tie onto the upright on the jetty.

'We'll get this raft built today. Those fuckers can lie in the cabin if they want. I know the fucking tide is turning, but if they weren't such fuck-ups we'd have gotten this one out as well. Where are the logs you were supposed to be getting out?'

I went to the edge of the jetty and shouted down at him.

'I'm finished, Arkland. Resigned. I'm out. I want no more of it.'

'What are you talking about?'

'There'll be no logs. I sent the men back to the camp. I called off the police. It's over, Arkland. It's over, for Christ's sake.'

Even though the logs moved treacherously under him, Arkland lunged across them to the edge of the jetty. He grabbed my ankles, one in each hand, and yanked me over his head as if we were an acrobatic act that had gone wrong. I landed on the raft behind him, banging my head and my wrists as I landed. I scrambled to my feet, feeling the timber move in the water under me. We faced each other, four logs separating us. I kept moving, shuffling from log to log as Arkland came towards me.

'You stupid Mick fucker, Mahon. You've fucked up once too often.'

He steadied himself on a log and then lunged forward. I ran along the raft parallel to the jetty edge and then changed direction, scrambled across two more logs and dived at the steel girders supporting the jetty. The timber under my feet swirled away from the jetty so that as I grabbed the middle girder my feet slipped off the log. I hung on, the rusting metal digging into my palms, but my feet went under the water.

'Arkland. Bastard. You.'

It was Ilpe. He hadn't seen me below him, clinging to the frame of the jetty. He had a parang in his hand.

'Arkland. Bastard. You,' he shouted again. He must be drunk, I thought.

'Don't mess with me, Ilpe. Just get out of here,' Arkland shouted at him, pointing a finger.

'You bastard, Arkland. You messed my sister. You messed my sister. You know that. You killed her, you bastard you.'

He jumped off the jetty, sending a shudder through the raft of logs that almost knocked Arkland off his feet. Then in two strides he reached Arkland and hit him square across the head with the parang. Arkland dropped to one knee and Ilpe struck him again, behind the ear, severing it so that it lay beside his prone body like a bloodied rag. As the logs moved about I managed to get my feet out of the water and back onto one. I heaved myself up onto the jetty. My wrists were weakened but I grabbed the steel upright and used the cable to haul myself up.

'Mahon. You.'

Ilpe staggered across the logs towards me. I grabbed the cable and yanked it off the upright. I threw it away from me into the river. The raft opened out, the logs snapping open and closed like crocodile jaws. Shock swept across Ilpe's eyes and he teetered backwards. Then, trying to steady himself, he tumbled forward, lost his footing and slipped off the raft. His parang flew into the air as he went under. His fingers grappling with a log were the last things I saw as the logs closed over him. They stayed over him and moved towards the sea. Then the raft opened again further over and Arkland's body slithered off and it too was covered by the logs. His ear stayed on a little longer, but as the raft separated fully, that log spun too and the ear slithered into the river and was lost.

I took off my boots and my shirt. Then I dived in, away to the side of the scattered raft of logs. I wanted to be clean. I wanted to submerge myself. I came up gasping out in the middle of the river, feeling the pull of the turning tide. Soon it would be completely against me. I struck out towards the sea. I felt the rhythm of my swimming coming back. Years of training and competitions came back to me. Soon I had reached the confluence of the river and the incoming tide. I breasted the small breakers and kept making out to sea. I saw the tug. She had turned and was coming back towards me.

I had never felt stronger. I was a flying fish. I would go out there, out past the tug, out past the cargo ship. I would go on, to Labuan, to Hong Kong, Japan. And on. As far as my swimming would carry me. I had been a great swimmer. I remembered the cheers of schoolmates as I touched the poolside. Then the tears of victory as I stood on the rostrum and looked up to see Gerald, a boy, clapping his hands above his head.

I trod water and felt the tide pull me across towards the beach. The tug and the ship got further away from me. I had swum hard, but there was no getting away. I turned and bodysurfed towards the beach.

I crawled onto the sand, my wrists aching each time I put my weight on them. I sat against a great meranti log, its rough edges welcome support. Blood streaked from my shins to my feet where I had torn at the psoriasis rash. My breath came out in gulps. I lay my head against the log and sobbed.

The men had come to the edge of the jetty. They were looking for Arkland. Maybe they knew Ilpe was there too. One of them went back and looked in my Land Rover. Another spotted me and alerted the rest of the crew, pointing to me on the beach.

I would have to go back. I would have to face up to it. This time for certain. Three people were dead. The boy. Arkland. Ilpe. And I played a part in the deaths of all of them. There was no avoiding that. And Gerald? There was no avoiding that either. I got up and started to walk along the beach towards the wooden bridge where a big truck rumbled by with a load of logs. Meranti. Seraya. Kerning. The big trees.

EPILOGUE

Home

CHAPTER TWENTY

It took nearly three months to sort out affairs at Camp K4. Finally, Sergeant Merkat said the evidence was inconclusive, so he could not press any charges. I thought to myself, who's left anyway? They're all dead. Except me.

Embury came, looking furious, and I handed over the camp papers to him. We mothballed the plant. The concession was closed down, to let the dust settle. I imagine it's open again by now.

I wandered around for a while. A gecko without a tail. Embury told me to take some leave on full pay. I went to Hong Kong. I went to Bangkok. I lazed on a beach in Sri Lanka. Searwood offered me other postings. I thought about them, but couldn't get excited. I left the beach and went to the hills around Kandy. I wrote a letter of resignation under the verandah of a shrine to the Buddha as monsoon rain deluged down.

Another death brought me home in the end. This time my mother's. I made it home for that funeral and stood beside my father, sullen in the mizzle that didn't cease until the gravediggers put the cover over my mother's grave. When we got back to the house, I overheard Mrs Heaney say to Mick Gallagher that shame had killed my mother. What kind of mother was she who had reared a son who wouldn't come home for his brother's funeral? Worrying like that killed my mother, she said.

I often feel sad about Gerald, especially when the ceasefires came just two years after his death. And I knew I had a lot to do. I knew I had to stay. There could be no going away again. It was a vicious irony that I became what my mother would have wanted me to become only after her death.

But things are getting better. My psoriasis is under control at last. No sign of the red weals now, just faint dry markings, almost scars. I got a job teaching Maths and Engineering

Science at the Tech. I was lucky to arrive home just as a new government youth-training initiative was about to begin. My father lets me help around the house more now. I have taken over his role as chopper of kindling. He still brings home the short pieces of wood, but now I stand in the yard at weekends, splitting them and tossing them into the drum beside the coal bunker. Sometimes he stands beside me, but I don't feel threatened by that. Just comforted, as if I'm beginning to feel like we're at ease together. We talk more, even about things we never talked about.

I teach Dodds at the Tech. He's doing a HND in mechanical engineering. He talks to me about Gerald, telling me about meetings I should attend, marches I should be on, anniversaries and commemorations I should mark. But I realise Gerald's way is not my way. I am trying to make my own way in my own place. I feel young and old at the same time. I feel I'm starting all over again. I even met Bronagh McCann for lunch once. She was home because her sister Claire is having a baby in a few months time and she wanted to see what she looked like pregnant. It was good to have a laugh with her about that, and I promised her that if I went to London I would look her up.

I went to one meeting. Some students were forming a group on the environment and had heard I'd worked in the rainforest. I spoke at the meeting and they seemed pleased enough. Somebody asked me if I thought the destruction of the rainforest should stop. I replied that I wasn't sure, but probably yes.

I seem to have left that all behind, and it is only when I go to Brooke Park and sit among the oaks and limes that visions of the rainforest come up and I see the river in flood, the roads subsiding, the great trees being dragged into clearings for loading onto the Macks.

And then in the distance I see a boy, up near where the swings are, or on the grassy slope, about to join other boys in a game of football. He has put aside his blowpipe, he has set aside

the rattan he was plaiting. The deer go unstalked, the squirrel –
king of the forest – comes to watch him play.

And then I go home, to my father and the life we are slowly
building from scratch.